AF429503

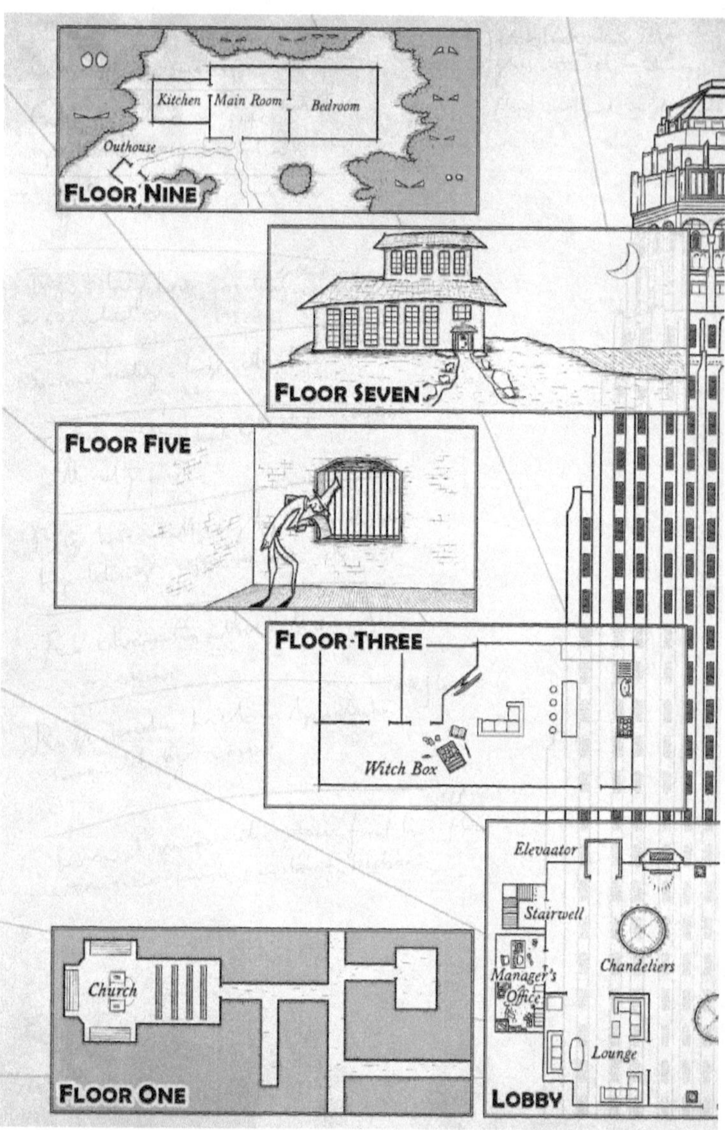

Kitchen
Main Room
Bedroom
Outhouse
FLOOR NINE
FLOOR SEVEN
FLOOR FIVE
FLOOR THREE
Witch Box
Church
FLOOR ONE
Elevaator
Stairwell
Manager's Office
Chandeliers
Lounge
LOBBY

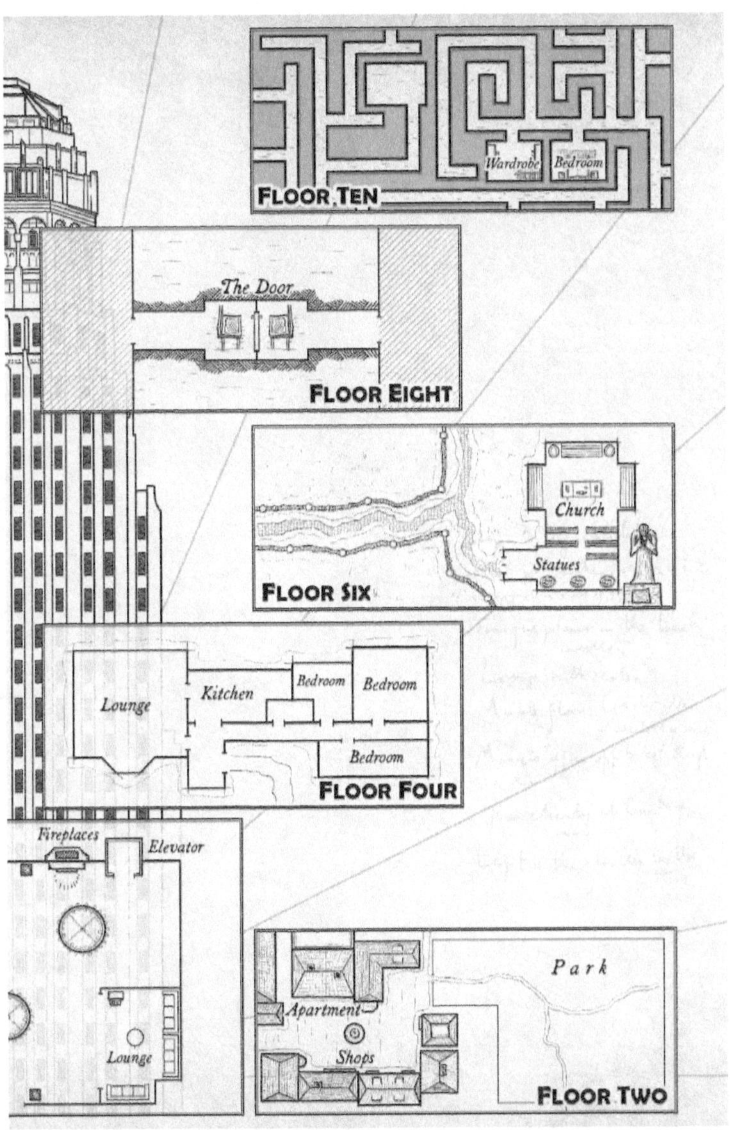

Fig. 1: The Hyperion
Map by Dewi Hargreaves

THE HYPERION
TALES FROM HELL

THE HYPERION
TALES FROM HELL

An anthology

Suzanna Lundale & Marc Tizura, *eds.*

For the ones who taught us the magic of wondering.

"Eternal fire, that inward burns, shows them with ruddy flame Illum'd."

    – Dante Alighieri, *The Divine Comedy*

"Within the bowels of these elements, where we are tortured and remain forever. Hell hath no limits, nor is circumscribed in one self place, for where we are is hell, and where Hell is must we ever be."

    – Christopher Marlowe, *Dr. Faustus*

Table of Contents

Foreword

The Hyperion started, as so many significant things do, with a spark. In February 2022, Marc Tizura, Founder & Co-Editor-in-Chief of End of the World Productions, was participating in a Twitter Writing Community activity, #fastprompt, whereby the moderator gives one prompt every 12 minutes for an hour, and participants write poems or stories to the prompts in real-time.

Marc conceived of a building that is sometimes located in his native Chicago, the residents of which are actually denizens of Hell. He thought how interesting it would be for a single character to speak to each resident and hear the stories of how they came to be there. It was a great idea, but an idea too big for a lone editor to pull off. He filed it away for Someday.

Fast forward to August of the same year. Through mutual friends in the Twitter Writing Community, Marc crossed paths with Suzanna Lundale enough times to start talking, as authors do, because, frankly, we're rather an obsessive lot, about projects they dreamed of doing. During one such confab, Marc told Suzanna about the building. Her immediate response was, "Let's do it."

Just over a year later, Marc and Suzanna have collected short stories and poems from fifteen other writers and poets from *four* continents to bring you The Hyperion: Tales from Hell, in which Brayden Winchell, a young urban explorer with some dark secrets, will confront the challenge of the legendary Hyperion building and, he hopes, live to tell the tale.

Readers will follow Brayden from resident to resident, hearing their stories and reading poetry as the writing on the walls in between. We are so excited to bring you this volume and share with you the wonderfully varied approaches our colleagues have taken. There is everything from classic horror tropes, rendered in full, shiver-inducing splendor, to deeply considered explorations of intention and the nature of fitting punishment, and so much else besides.

There are ideas, both grim and light-hearted, about Hell that many cultures carry among the fixtures of our shared libraries of reference – the flames, the torment, the humiliation, like that often seen when Adolf Hitler is depicted enjoying the hospitality of Hell – but among them have always tiptoed interesting outliers.

There is, for example, the allegory of the long spoons, attributed to, among others, Rabbi Haim of Romshishok, which has become part of folk culture of many cultures in the East, Middle East, and West. The story posits that people in Hell are given spoons too long to feed themselves, so they starve forever, while people in Heaven are given the same spoons and use them to feed each other.

There is Aldous Huxley's idea that "[m]aybe this world is another planet's Hell," and Jean-Paul Sartre's widely misunderstood assertion that "Hell is other people." There is Neil Gaiman's more post-religious idea that "Hell is something you carry around with you. Not somewhere you go."

There may be as many versions of Hell and its mechanisms as there are people who have thought about it. Clearly, Hell is an idea that still fascinates. Our hope is that the reader will come away with new ideas, and new questions. New things to wonder. We hope you enjoy the stories and poems we have collected here. And now, turn the page, and join us. Welcome to The Hyperion. We've been expecting you.

A note about spelling and grammar standards: While both editors live in the United States, we were keen to avoid making American English a normative default for this volume. As such, each piece has been carefully edited and proofread according to the standards of that contributor's country of residence.

Welcome to The Hyperion

The building loomed ominously against the night sky, a jutting black monolith of glass and steel.

It made Brayden Winchell feel small. He despised it for that.

It had appeared at the corners of Thorndale and Sheridan, where the former dead ends and becomes Thorndale Beach, in the Edge Water neighborhood of Chicago.

Brayden ran his fingers over the thirteen notches on his belt, rapidly muttering their mantra under his breath – a mantra for no one else's ears but his own. As he drew nearer, he had an impression of the building as a massive black dog, vicious if awakened.

What he had been told his whole life about letting sleeping dogs lie, well, that wasn't his style, was it? Thankfully, he hadn't started recording yet. He didn't want his followers to see a moment of doubt.

Brayden turned on his camera and placed it in the cradle on his chest. He cleared his throat and began to speak.

"Well, here it is, the mother fucking Hyperion! Who's ready to go into this bitch? Spooks? Specters? I don't think so. Let's debunk some myths and solve this mystery!" Brayden started for the door.

To get to it, he walked over the cracked and crumbling cobblestones of the front courtyard, past a cracked marble fountain, long since out of order. Stagnant black water lay on the floor of the basin.

To the left of the doors, running the length of the large picture window, sat a concrete planter full of dead plants and a black metal sign.

The building's name was spelled out in white lights reading:

"The Hyperion"

Before Brayden went in, he stroked the side of the building; it felt warm, even alive, to his touch. Almost like human skin. He ran nervous fingers over his belt, took a deep breath, and grabbed the bar of the revolving door.

Brayden Winchell entered The Hyperion.

The lobby was cavernous. Three huge glass chandeliers hung in a row, from the front door to the back wall, responsible for most of the light in the room. Smaller spotlight bulbs ran along the ceiling's perimeter, though a fair number had burned out.

Two massive planters flanked the entrance, mirrored by their twins at the back wall. All the plants inside them were dead.

The walls bore dark wood paneling, a generic-looking relic from either the fifties or the seventies, Brayden thought.

Twin lounge areas were arrayed in front of the two large picture windows on either side of the entrance. Exhausted couches and chairs had collapsed in on themselves, with pieces of wood and metal springs jutting out. The tables were grimy and stained. Twin fireplaces sat cold, long since dormant.

A thick layer of dust caked nearly every surface in the lobby. Spiderwebs and cobwebs hung in corners and fixtures all over.

At the center of the lobby crouched a circular desk for door staff or a concierge. Brayden crossed the marble floor to stand in front of it.

The granite top stood on a sturdy wooden base. Drawers and cabinets hung open, doors askew; clipboards holding tattered papers were stacked haphazardly atop the cabinets. A broken office chair sat empty in the middle. A large, clunky phone resembling a payphone sat next to a comically large monitor screen positioned in the doorman's line of sight with the door.

A dusty sign read, "Back in five minutes." Brayden scoffed. He doubted that.

A noise to his left brought his head up with a jerk. A door stood open, through which he spied a desk, a stack of boxes, and papers strewn about.

Probably the manager's office, Brayden thought.

He thought there was movement at the back of the office, like a shadow. His fingers went unbidden to the notches on his belt.

He felt watchful eyes on him. Not a single pair, but many. Thousands of them, each one full of hate and insanity. A sound like a deep, rumbling laugh seemed to come from the office. The air felt electrified. He broke out in gooseflesh.

"Oh, fuck you!" he growled to the empty lobby.

At once, the sensation stopped and the air stilled. His gooseflesh receded. The noise was just rats, the shadow was a trick of the light, and the rest was his overactive imagination.

"Fuck you," he said again to the empty lobby.

He marched to the back wall where twin elevators sat waiting, more determined than ever to debunk the mystery and mystique of this place.

Not surprisingly, the elevators were not operational. One car had fallen to the first floor from a considerable height, it seemed, and smashed. A frayed cable lay among chunks of broken car on the floor in front of it.

The other car was stuck midway between the lobby and first floor. He could put his hands on the floor of the car and look in, but there wasn't enough room to climb up and into it. He took his camera and filmed the interior of the car.

He peered down to the floor below. It was cement and farther down than he'd expected. Long, metal-cased electrical wires coiled out from a box along one wall. Three metal prongs jetted out of it. Brayden whistled, imagining what it would be like to fall on those.

A thunderous crack was his only warning before part of the ceiling broke loose and crashed to the floor just behind him. Brayden jumped, nearly falling forward into the open shaft. Only quick reflexes earned over a lifetime playing sports saved him.

He shot both hands out, gripping the sides of the outer door and saving himself from a nasty tumble. His heart raced like a jackhammer. He let out several slow, shaky breaths. When he felt calm and more sure-footed, he let go and slowly backed away from the elevator over a floor left uneven by the chunk of ceiling debris that almost did him in.

What began as a nervous laugh grew bolder until it became a cheer, and then a whoop. He stuck his middle finger up in defiance and made a slow circle around the lobby.

"Nice try, asshole!" he called out to whatever was running this place. He ran his fingers over his belt notches to ground himself.

It would have to be the stairs. To the left of the two dead elevators was a sign on a wood panel reading, "Stairs."

Brayden walked over and pushed. The panel gave way, opening onto a dimly lit stairwell. Brayden began his ascent.

At the top of the first flight, he saw a single door at the end of a long hallway. "Let's see what's behind door number one," he said, starting down the dingy hall. As he went, he became aware that the plaster on one wall was cracking as he went.

Brayden's steps faltered as he watched the cracks become letters. The letters began to fill with... something that looked a lot like blood. Was it blood? The scent of copper assailing his nose confirmed that it must be.

The blood pooled, filling the letters to their edges, but never running over. Brayden began to read.

Allegory
C.E. Wallace

Misshapen forms dance
   on barren walls
brushstrokes of madness
     paint spectral
hands that echo
    cries of
  TICK
   TOCK

days pass, hours
inch and
shadows
  l e n g t h e n
gross
    distortions
of darkness
    grim omens
of life and
    death

within penumbral edges
          tenuous luminescence
holds court
          over darkness
marking liminal
                    passage
                              between
obscurity and
          enlightenment

for what are
          shadows but the
suggestion of
          light
a lesson in perception

1. A Different Light
Jessica Laymon

A flock of shrill morning birds called as David got out of his car that Sunday morning. He slammed the car door in annoyance and winced. Rubbing his temples and squinting at the sun, which was just beginning to peek its golden rays over the ridge, he made a beeline toward the front door of the church and the relative darkness inside. He was early, but he liked to have the place to himself for a while. He shuffled his way quickly toward the yellow-bricked church, a sour expression on his face.

Digging for his keys, he dropped them twice before fitting the right one into the lock. His wife had kindly put a green cover on the top of the key so he wouldn't forget, but color coordination had never been his strong suit. He cursed under his breath when the key didn't fit the first time, but once he got it into the worn keyhole, he nearly broke it in his haste to get inside, away from the punishing bright of the dawning sun.

The hallways were dark, and the padded carpets blessedly muffled his footsteps as he made his slow way to his office. He bumped into a wall on his way in and nearly fell, but once he was in his chair, he sat back with a sigh. Loud birds and bright sun forgotten, David was free to muse that morning really was the best time, at least, in his estimation.

The air outside was just slightly crisp on this Fall morning, which eased his frayed nerves. One deep breath of cold air, and he could forget about all his problems for a time. *His problems. Damn.* Just like that, they all came rushing back. He groaned.

Desperate to regain even part of his morning peace, David pulled open a drawer. "Now where did I put that thing?" he muttered partly to himself, partly to anyone listening. In truth, he half-wanted to be caught. He was terrified someone would notice, but at the same time, he *did not care.*

Rummaging in the drawer for a moment, he finally found it, shoved at the back of a pile of old kids' drawings. The bottle knocked into the side of the drawer with a small tinkle as he pulled it out, unscrewed the lid, and took a long, generous pull. Some of his problems began and ended with little bottles much like this one, but unlike at home, at the church, he only had the one stash.

"A little spirit to soothe the spirit. You don't mind, do you? I've had a hell of a week." It wasn't like *He* was actually listening, not now. David knew that the face of God was turned away from him, and why shouldn't it be? He was *the* omnipresent and omnipotent God. He knew and saw all, and so He knew all about David's transgressions.

Being a pastor made it worse, of course. He was the spiritual leader of the people who went to this church. He should be strong in the face of the Enemy. And he should damn well set a good example for the children. All Nadine's words, and they tumbled around in his head like lottery balls. Didn't she know what the Bible had to say about wives obeying their husbands? He raised the bottle to drink.

A confident knock rattled through the hollow office door. David stilled, bottle painfully close to his lips, hoping he had imagined it. The knock sounded again, followed by a strong male voice. "I know you're in there. I heard you. Not like you have anywhere to run, right?"

David stared at the door. Failing a figment of his fevered imagination, he'd expected his wife, come to nag him further before services. He raised the bottle the rest of the way and took a swift pull. He started to rise to send whoever it was away with a threat of police, if need be.

The door opened, and a tall, athletic young man entered, a sneer on his face. David spluttered impotently as the young man examined the two chairs in front of the desk with distaste before settling lightly on the edge of one of them.

"Who are you?" demanded David. "How did you get in here?" Had he forgotten to lock the door behind him when he entered? Possibly. Still, that was hardly an invitation. He settled back into his chair, glowering at the newcomer.

"I'm Brayden Winchell," the young man said, with a smug finality that suggested the name should mean something to him.

"Good to know, so I can tell the police. What are you, some kind of missionary? Did my wife send you?"

Brayden laughed. "Sure, let's go with missionary. I'm here to hear your story, *padre*. How did you get here?"

"How did I get here?" David echoed. "I drove, like everybody does."

"No, I mean, how did you get *here*, to The Hyperion? What happened? What did you have to do? Did you get an invitation?"

David snorted at the idea of an invitation and took another pull from the whiskey bottle he still held. He sat back, and looked around the small office, contemplating the missionary's question. In another two hours, the stillness would be shattered by the screaming of toddlers and babies, the stomping of the older kids' feet as they ran up and down the rickety, green-carpeted stairs that led to the children's Sunday school classes, and the loud cackles of laughter of his older parishioners.

So much life, but none of it for him. They told more jokes when he wasn't around (or was *he* the joke?) it seemed like, but perhaps that was just his imagination. In the meantime, he was apparently drinking himself into a stupor. He thought of Nadine's likely reaction and took a long drink. *Nadine.*

"You want to know what kind of invitation I got? I got a threat from my wife last night. She actually threatened *me*! Said she'd go to the board and get my license to preach stripped from me if I didn't straighten up my act. The woman is insane." David seethed anew remembering her quiet anger. She had to be insane. Why else would she threaten him that way? Didn't she know how hard it was being a leader of men?

"Sure, after she caught me the first time, she was forgiving and lenient." *And yet*, he mused to himself, *somehow, Shelly was never invited to church functions after that and apparently moved away sometime later.* "Nadine was never once angry with me. She told me that the sin was wicked, but it was all because I'd let myself be tempted. She said she knew that if I prayed about it, God would help me find a way."

So he'd dropped to his knees then and there and prayed, or pretended to, and she'd left him alone. There were tears in her eyes when she left the room.

"It's all her fault!" He yelled into the quiet, no longer even acknowledging Brayden's presence. "All her fault!" If she'd graced their marriage bed with her presence, with the intention of fulfilling her wifely duties, then he wouldn't have had those needs. He wouldn't have had to find someone else to fill her role. "Her fault," he whispered and killed the last of the bottle.

The room tilted around him, and David closed his eyes. He was drunk at church, but he didn't care anymore. Let them tell the board! Let them get him removed. Maybe he'd take up something more worthwhile afterward. Maybe he'd go find Shelly.

With a jolt, he came out of his sulking reverie and sat up. "Who's there?" Hadn't there been someone...? He was alone now, the door to his office open. He could have sworn he heard the front door open and close. He rubbed his eyes, his vision blurred. Had he passed out? What time was it? He pulled his phone out of his pocket and opened it to check the time. Dead. Figured.

David looked out the window, but there was no one else parked out front. The glass pane still felt cool to the touch as he rested his head against it; it eased the headache somewhat. It had been clear when he arrived, but now the sky was heavily overcast. He wished it was pouring rain instead.

For one thing, it made it difficult to tell just how long he'd slept, and for another, he always felt better when it rained. There was nothing like a good heavy downpour, washing away everything. He could walk out in it and claim that he'd stopped to help someone change a tire. He pulled a mint out of his pocket and stuck it in his mouth.

He caught his reflection as he turned. The large, old mirror was a holdover from a previous pastor that he hadn't convinced anyone to help him throw out. It was a heavily-framed, old-fashioned thing that looked as though it was purchased from a second-hand store in the '70s. Looking closer at his face in the dim light, he realized he looked like hell. Shadows decorated his face, some from his unshaven cheeks, and his eyes looked hollow, sunken. Not exactly the image of the neighborhood pastor.

"Handsome as ever," he groaned. He winked ironically at his reflection and turned to leave the office. It was as good a time as any.

"Aaaaaaaaaahhhhhh!"

The wordless bellow made David dive for cover, hunkering behind the wall next to the door. He opened and closed his mouth, wiped his face, and tried to tell himself he was letting his imagination run away with him. That deep voice! That cadence! That timbre! He was frozen to the spot, convinced someone was playing a trick *and* that he was losing his mind. Was he dreaming? He pinched himself.

"Ouch!" Okay, that was too hard. He stuck his hand in his mouth. Should he get up and see what was going on? Was it better to stay right here, to not move, and to let someone else find whatever it was? Or for them to find him huddled on the floor, mumbling incoherently?

What the- Brayden's exploration to see how far the church set-up went was halted by an impossibly loud voice bellowing somewhere past the preacher's office. Cautiously, he made his way back in that direction. At the door to the sanctuary, he stopped. A giant black... *thing* hulked there with an air of waiting. Brayden had never seen anything like it. The special effects in this place were crazy good. When the preacher pushed past him to confront the thing, Brayden grinned in anticipation.

A thump and a crash seemed to rock the walls, and David scrambled to his feet. Trembling, he walked back to his desk, quiet as a mouse, and pulled open another drawer. Inside was a revolver, his one holdout from a time spent on the wrong side of life, before he'd been called to serve. His hands trembled as he flipped open the chamber and pulled out several shiny bullets, stuffing them into the holes with perhaps too much force.

Clicking it shut, he crept out of his office, not bothering to shut the door behind him. Nothing could have prepared him for what he found when he entered the chapel.

Dark wings spread to either side of the hall. A... being that was all blackness glared at him with glowing red eyes. Horns seemed to stretch from its head and touch the ceiling, but the thing was all shadows. David stopped where he stood, mouth slack. The gun nearly fell from his limp fingers. He tightened his grip, but found no strength to move.

"You come," the demon said. There was no mouth, just a voice in his head. He dropped to his knees, clutching his skull. Its voice reverberated through his mind, and he saw a scattering of colors there, like stained glass shattering. Colors swam, and he grew dizzy.

"What..." David stood shakily and shuffled a little further into the chapel. A part of his brain begged him to run, but he could not. The darkness pulsed in front of where the Sunday school children usually sang, and *it* seemed to sing to him, to pull him forward.

"It's time to call you to account, sinner." The voice carried a hint of dark mirth. **"You died hours ago in your office. Alcohol poisoning, they'll suppose."** David shook his head, as much in denial as to try to shake the horrible voice from his head. **"Someone found your lifeless body. A child. Fitting, no?"** This had to be a nightmare, or hallucination. David reached up and felt his chest. His pulse was strong, and too fast, perhaps, but he was definitely still breathing.

"Liar!" He moved toward the beastly darkness, unable to halt himself, as if he were being pulled by an invisible force toward the creature. It dwarfed the room, engulfed the end of it, a pulsing pitch blackness that seemed to drink in all light.

"Am I? Is not this your personal hell?" A part of the darkness shifted, as though waving a hand around. **"To be trapped forever where you were not wanted, were not loved, were not respected? To know that you were never good enough to lead?"** There was a cacophonous chuckle that seemed to shake the walls around it.

"You were never like your father, never good enough for him. He always found fault in you. So you claimed to be called, became a pastor, like him, to prove him wrong. Now you're stuck here for all eternity."

"No. I don't believe you," David panted. He was halfway down the aisle and had to look up into the demon's red eyes. Its wings drooped around behind him. He felt them pushing against his back.

"You wanted out. I *know* you, David. I've been within you all along, and I know you craved a life that wasn't your own, girls that weren't for you. You tried to do what you wanted, and now you must pay."

David laughed. "Shouldn't you be encouraging those things, if you're a demon, and not some trick of my imagination?"

"I did encourage you, sinner. I've been with you since your beginning. It was I who suggested you blame the girl. She wasn't like that before you got to her, was she? But

after?" The thing took a great breath. **"Ah, now that was art."**

"She was calling my name, calling me to come to her!"

"All in your mind, David. She was screaming for you to stop. Her parents took her to therapy after that, but she was never right again. A few years later, she was found floating in her bathtub. Should I tell you about the track marks up and down her arms? The miscarriages? No? What else then…?"

The thing reached out its arms as though to gather David to it. He was overwhelmed by a rushing darkness, like falling into a dark pit. He pointed his gun at its dark visage, and it laughed. **"Try to kill me, if you want. Try."** It took a heavy step toward him, and the church floor rocked. David pulled back the hammer on the revolver…

"David? Why are you pointing a gun at me?" The lights flared suddenly, and Nadine was walking up the aisle, her blonde hair cascading around her like a halo. But he couldn't halt his finger. He'd aimed at the demon, and now…

The hammer came down and the bullet flew true. He dropped the gun and immediately started running, as though he could stop it in mid-air, as though he were somehow fast enough to stop it. "No!!!"

He could hear people gathering behind him and heard their gasps of horror. Someone grabbed him from behind and wrestled him to the floor. He tried to reach for the gun, but someone else kicked it away.

His wife's still form lay a few paces away, her eyes open in surprise, in accusation. "But he said I was already dead!" David screamed.

Somewhere, in the distance, he heard a low, rumbling laugh.

Shaken by how real it all felt – the creature, the shot, the dead wife, the broken man wrestled down by his own parishioners, Brayden stood rooted to the spot. Until he heard the laughter. The preacher went perfectly still in his captors' arms, as if he had heard it, but the others didn't react. *What the-*

Brayden turned and fled the scene, pulling the door behind him with relief at finding himself back in the dim hallway of The Hyperion. He headed for the stairs.

Rounding the corner at the top of the flight, he stepped onto the second floor. Dead ahead stood the door. He reflected that this hallway was, if anything, more dimly lit than the one below.

He walked briskly until he felt his shoes moving through something wet and squishy. Before he could adjust his pace, one shoe slipped. He shot out a hand to catch himself, but jerked back when it encountered cold moisture on the wall.

Brayden shone his light along the ground, and himself, to discover that the floor, his shoes, and his hand were covered in what appeared to be blood. He let out a groan of disgust.

Then he saw them, the words carved into the wall, bleeding freely down the wall and onto the floor.

Untitled
Uchechkwu Onyedikam

memory sinks her teeth
deeply into the thought
of wild imaginings
making monsters
of fairies in my sleep

2. Just a Small Town Girl

RT Slaywood

Brayden Winchell stood on the sidewalk of the street, or at least, what was supposed to represent a sidewalk. He had expected the room to be big, as there was only one door on this level, but he hadn't expected how big. Now that he was inside, he had trouble wrapping his tired mind around the actual size of this room.

It looked like a small town.

Stepping inside, his awe turned to panic. Immediately, he spun on his heel and lunged, fully committed to catching the door before it closed, but was too late. Dread fought against his own stupidity as he tried the door anyway.

"Locked."

He groaned as he rested his head against the solid wood. Closing his eyes, he took a deep breath and made a mental note to bring an ax on his next exploration. He took a moment to think back to just before he opened the door and came inside. He'd had a clear plan to prop the door open this time, just in case. Why hadn't he remembered?

"This damned building," he said to himself as he banged his fist into the door next to his head.

He felt the reverberation in his skull, which helped purge the fleeting superstition, along with a second deep breath. Normally, these expeditions have zero encounters with other people, but after seeing the directory and the previous floor, he realized he wanted to know what this floor had in store for him. His other hand went from rubbing the notches on his belt to flicking open his camera as he prepared to go back through the footage to review the names on the directory.

A black eye was watching him through the peephole.

A second wave of fear took over him. He startled back with a shout, but quickly turned it to cursing as his courage took back over. In a single motion, he hit record and pressed his camera to the peephole, then checked himself a moment later.

"Nothing, fuck!" Hands shaking from the adrenaline, he brought up the camera and played back the footage, hoping to catch proof of what he saw.

Nothing.

Grumbling unintelligibly, Brayden turned around and leaned against the door, looking at the indoor town again before beginning his walkthrough.

"Okay, I'm on the second floor now. As you can see, this unit is massive." He chuckled to himself to ease his nerves. "The buildings here are reminiscent of a small, middle-America town, and judging by this hollowed-out Volkswagen Beetle, my guess is the time it was intended to capture was sometime in the 1980s.

"As you can see, we have streetlamps, a radio station, a post office, a fire hydrant, even a barber/hair salon, but the whole façade falls apart when you look up." He pointed the camera at the ceiling. "The steel rafters have been painted black and the lack of lighting makes me think this room is in an eternal state of nighttime."

Nearing the park, Brayden stopped and tsked. Now, in what he guessed was the center of the small town, he saw one of his least favorite things to find while exploring.

Mannequins.

He put on a cheerful voice, despite his own misgivings about the décor, and continued his tour. "Best part is, this cozy abode features dozens of residents, so you'll never feel alone!" He walked up to one for a close-up. "This one comes complete with a ball cap, sweats, and..." he paused as he noticed something large in the pocket. Stepping to the side, he lowered the camera to his waist level to get the best shot. "Drumroll please..." he said as he rolled his tongue, and prayed it wasn't something disgusting.

Or dangerous.

It was leather.

"A wallet!" he said triumphantly, producing the pocket's contents for his future audience. One-handed, he flipped it open and began taking inventory, set to get it all in one shot. "This one's name is David...Chrisman..." Despite himself, Brayden started to feel the unease of his discovery as he talked. Unlike the rest of the town, this wallet was real. A real ID, real cash and credit cards, real pictures of his wife. Hell, even rewards cards and insurance.

"Well, David, if you see this, send me a DM proving this is yours and I'll be sure to send it back to you."

Brayden stuffed the wallet into his pocket and continued the tour. "Let's step over to this café and see if we can get some food!"

Motion in the café window caught his attention.

In the window sat a beautiful woman with long, wavy black hair, drinking a coffee. She hadn't seen him yet, as her eyes appeared to be locked on something in the distance, away from where he was standing. Keeping the video on her, he tracked her line of sight to a large white building made to look like stone. Above the columns, carved in stone, was the word "Courthouse," and above that, a large clock. It only had two hands, so it was hard to tell if it was moving, but currently, it was on 5:55.

Brayden checked his phone, which confirmed the same time.

Has it really been almost 3 hours already?

He looked back and froze.

She was looking at him now.

The seconds that passed between them felt like an eternity. Cold sweat broke out on his neck and his heart sounded louder than before as he realized he had forgotten to review the directory to figure out what her name was. Would she be friendly?

Would she attack? More than most, Brayden knew that looks could be deceiving, and for all he knew, she could have written any number of the disturbing messages on the walls he had passed. It wouldn't be his first time having to defend himself against some squatter or druggie who seemed normal at first glance.

His fingers brushed his belt notches while he considered grabbing his mace.

The moment passed as she broke eye contact first and returned to drinking her coffee and watching the clock.

"Looks like we have another resident," Brayden said, walking towards the café door. For all intents and purposes, it looked like a fake café. The building was painted all white, with two windows flanking the door, which was propped open. Above the door was the building's label in a large, plain black font.

Having walked through the door, Brayden found the inside wasn't much better. The tables and chairs were cheap iron topped with wood laminate, the kind that would stick to your arms if rested on for too long. There was a single mannequin behind the brushed steel counter, dressed in blue jeans and an apron-covered polo.

The woman by the window to his left didn't move, giving Brayden time to think about how to approach her. "Well, let's get a coffee shall we?" he said, deciding to play along with whatever was going on. Stepping up to the counter, he noted the name tag on the mannequin, Hunter, before looking at the chalkboard menu behind him while tapping on the counter.

"Well, Hunter, I'll have a—" Brayden stopped mid-sentence, noticing the drink already sitting on his side of the counter, with what was probably a misspelled name on the side. "Never mind, looks like you already got it!" he finished, and grabbed the drink. Stepping to an empty table, he put his camera down and lifted the lid.

The strong scent of coffee smelled fresh. The drizzle of caramel floated on foam that had yet to dissolve into the drink. He took a sip for the camera.

"Caramel Macchiato, for sure. Good guess, Hunter."

"You forgot to pay." Brayden jumped at the sternness of the woman's voice. Thankfully, she was still watching the clock from her seat at the window and hadn't decided to walk up to him while he was absorbed in the mysterious drink's appearance. Brayden admonished himself as he walked back to the counter, making sure to keep his attention on her as he did.

"Yeah, sorry about that. My bad." He reached into his pocket and pulled the bills from the wallet without taking it out, removed a $5, and placed it on the counter. "Keep the change."

Going back to his camera and drink, he grabbed both before walking over to her window-side seat. On the way, he dropped the camera on a nearby table to record his interview. Step by step, he considered several ways to start a conversation. Everything from a bad joke, to being new in town, to diving straight into asking about The Hyperion.

Brayden decided to wing it as he took the last step up next to her table. Now, standing next to her, he realized just how beautiful she was. She was about his age. Her dark black hair framed her lightly freckled face. A simple gold locket hung from her neck that matched her gold hoop earrings. Her blouse was unbuttoned just enough to—

"Can I help you?" Her green eyes dug holes into his, all the way down to his chest, causing his heart to skip a beat.

Despite himself, Brayden felt embarrassed. "Ah, sorry. I just didn't expect to meet anyone else here."

"Funny, considering coffee shops are usually busy in the morning," she replied. "But that doesn't excuse looking down my shirt."

He could feel heat rising up his face, forcing him to break eye contact. Instead, he looked out the window while he tried to think of what to say. *I'm definitely going to have to edit that part out; otherwise, I'm going to get canceled.*

"Well?"

"Yeah, sorry, I'm new in town and—"

"Again, great story, but has nothing to do with you being rude."

Brayden looked back to her and his thoughts screeched to a halt.

"Uh..."

Her eyes widened slightly as her head shook in an attempt to get him to spit it out.

"So..." she nodded for him to continue.

"So did you ever hear about the two muffins in an oven?" He screamed internally as her expression changed from hopeful to done.

"No, and I don't have time for jokes," she said, grabbing her coffee and standing. "I have shopping to do."

As Brayden watched her throw away her cup and leave, he wondered what in the hell had come over him. Once she was gone, he wordlessly went back to his camera, turned off the recording, and drank his coffee as he stared out the window. Aside from the blunder with this floor's resident, and the creepy mannequins, he was thankful it was relatively calm compared to the previous floor. Still, something was off.

Though he was thankful that the coffee was his favorite, he began to wonder what the chances were that it would be. Glancing back at the chalkboard menu, he counted the number of possible orders and figured it was, at best, a one out of eight chance. The math only deepened his sense that something was out of place. He considered possible explanations, like maybe it was the woman's favorite drink as well. He resolved to go check the trash to see what her cup had written on it.

Written.

Brayden looked at the cup in his hand. His mouth went dry as he realized it was his name written in black sharpie on the side.

"Braydon." Misspelled, just as he had quipped... silently.

That revelation was cut short as a second thought finally made its way to the front of his mind.

Hunter was gone.

Unease turned to fear as that realization took center stage in Brayden's mind. What had started with his feeling that something was off, had gnawed at his subconscious until he found what had changed. Brayden glanced at the counter. Nothing. The hair on his neck stood on end and his hearing sharpened as he looked around for any sign of someone else, but it was hard to focus, knowing something or someone had moved it. He stood, chair screeching on the concrete floor as he grabbed his camera with one hand and his baton with the other. Turning on the record button, he mentally fell back on his content creator persona above all else.

"Well guys, you will not believe this, but it looks like we're not alone here." He backed out of the café. "Someone moved the barista while my back was turned." Outside the building, he turned, scanning the other buildings' labels. Finding the one labeled "Market," he continued.

"But that's okay, because, 'Safety first,'" he said, flicking his wrist to extend his baton. "Unfortunately, my battery ran out before I could interview this apartment resident, but now I'm fully charged and ready to go." Despite his tone and demeanor, Brayden felt panic edging its way into his mind. He pushed it out with determination.

Get the content and get out.

He walked towards the market, eyeing the farther streets and storefronts for any sign of a third party, but came up short. The woman was still inside the small store, which was about the size of a large gas station market. Short metal shelves filled with generic renditions of basic goods gave the feeling of being in a play market and increased Brayden's sense of unease. That, and the number of mannequins in the store. In addition to the clerk and floor employee mannequins, there were six shopper mannequins posed in various stages of shopping.

Nearby, one shopper was set up in mid-grab of an iconic yellow bag of chips, labeled simply, "Chips." Next to the counter, a mannequin dressed in a sundress had a cart half-full of vegetables that looked so fresh, they seemed unreal. Near the back, one had the door open to the fridge case as it reached for a gallon of milk.

It felt crowded.

Yet in the middle of it all, the woman went about her shopping as if nothing was amiss. She pushed her cart, checking prices and labels, and even said, "Excuse me," as she passed a mannequin bent over the meat case. Watching her, Brayden felt his panic fade into ridiculousness. He had come here to solve the mystery of The Hyperion, and what? Gotten scared the second something mysterious happened?

No way.

He walked up to the woman. "Hey, I'm sorry for before. My name is Brayden Winchell. I'm an urban explorer looking into the mystery of this building. I was wondering if you had time to talk about The Hyperion?"

For a moment, he thought she was ignoring him, until she huffed and began to answer. "Well, Mr. Muffinman, you must be dumber than you look," she said as she grabbed a square blue package labeled "Cookies," and put it in her cart.

"Fair enough, so since you're talking, can I assume that means you agree to giving an interview?"

"Sure, but I'm not going to stop what I'm doing for this. I would like to get home before everyone wakes up."

"Right," he said, bringing the camera up to eye level. "So can you first tell me your name?"

"Marri."

"Marri what?"

"I'm not giving you my last name."

"Fair, fair." *Not that I can't look it up in the directory. Though I guess that means she won't tell me what year she was born.* "So, Marri, how did you end up...living here?"

"Same as everyone, The Hyperion found me," she said as she finished her shopping and walked to the checkout. Brayden let her lead a distance before circling around in front of her.

"How did that go?"

She talked as she put her items on the counter one by one before putting them into bags she had brought herself. "I had outgrown the small town I grew up in and thought it was time for a change. I moved to Chicago. Got some work. But my first apartment was terrible." Finished, she put her cart away, grabbed her bags, and began to leave. "Let's talk in the park."

Brayden followed her, admiring her walk as she went. She wore a nice sundress, much like the one the mannequin in the store had been wearing, and it fit her nicely. Under different circumstances, he would probably try to hit on her, at least a little.

She put her bags down next to the bench, then sat facing the courthouse clock that now read 6:15. Brayden sat next to her and continued filming her profile.

"Then one day I got a letter that made it clear that this is where I would live."

"You wouldn't happen to still have that, would you?"

"I might, back at my apartment."

"Isn't this your apartment?"

She looked at him, into the camera, and pushed a stray lock of hair behind her ear. "Ah, yeah, that's right. I meant where I sleep here."

Brayden knew he had touched on something, but didn't want to have her cut him off so soon. "So, what made you think you outgrew your hometown?" he asked, before glancing around to make sure no one had moved any other mannequins.

"It was a really small town, only a couple hundred people, and by the time I was 30, I realized nothing had changed." She paused before looking back to the clock. "I had gotten too comfortable. After that, I had to leave."

Brayden felt a pang of familiarity at that. "I get that. I grew up in Highland Park, and nothing ever happened there, either. Wasn't until I started exploring that my life really started."

She smiled at that. "So, how did you start exploring?"

"It started with a hazing, actually!" He laughed. "It was freshman year of high school and I had tried out for football, because what guy wouldn't? After I was accepted, they called us out to an abandoned house that was supposedly haunted by the ghost of a serial killer and all his victims."

"Was it?"

"No, of course not. I passed through their test of courage with flying colors. After that, though, I realized how much fun I had going through that old house. Feeling history. I started watching YouTube videos, then started making my own."

She laughed lightly and shifted to better face him. "You're braver than you look, to have come here knowingly."

"Yeah, a bit, I guess you could say that." Brayden laughed a little as well. "Did you know anything about this place before coming here?"

"Me? No, not really. Though I had a dream about it before I decided to move. I think that's why I ended up coming to Chicago."

"What happened in your dream?"

"I'd had a really long day before, so it's hard to remember everything. I didn't even remember the dream until I came here in person after getting my letter."

"You had said that the letter made it clear you would live here. What did you mean?"

"What?" She smiled and tilted her head. "Oh, I just meant that it was obvious I would live here, because it looked so nice and was affordable."

Right.

She looked at the clock before turning away from him. "Well, that's about all the time I have, unfortunately. I have to get my ice cream home before it melts," she said as she grabbed her bags and stood. "We'll have to finish this another day."

Even a guy like Brayden could tell she was done with the interview. "Yeah, that's fair. I'm probably going to head out." He said, rising with her. His readiness to get away from the mannequins fought with the drive to get more information that could lead him to better answers before he left The Hyperion. In the end, the latter won. "Though I was wondering if I could see that letter before I leave?"

She turned, glancing nervously at the clock before looking at him. "Uh, I guess. I've never had someone see where I live before though, so it's a bit messy."

"That's fine. I can wait outside your apartment when you go to grab it."

"Sure, but only if you promise not to peek," she said as she turned and began walking through the fake little town once more.

Brayden was relieved to see the number of mannequins decreasing as they neared her apartment. It was a small two-level building far from the original entrance, whose roof reached up into the painted rafters. The play-like style of the town made the large building feel unstable, but Brayden was determined to get his evidence from this floor before leaving. Inside, there were two doors on either side and a single staircase that went up to the second level. There, on the landing, was a lone mannequin dressed as a mailman. They walked up the stairs to the only numbered apartment.

Apartment 5.

Brayden peaked periodically down the staircase to make sure the mailman wouldn't disappear as Marri fished out her keys to open the door. Finally, she opened it and said, "You know what, I don't mind if you come inside while I look for it."

The inside of Marri's apartment was vastly different from the rest of the town. The things in here felt like someone actually lived in the unit. Brayden realized it was the small details that made the difference. A small rug to wipe your feet on. The basket hung next to the door for her keys. House plants. Extra pairs of shoes. Pictures on the walls. All of it made it feel like a home. To his right, he could look out on the small town, which from this angle looked like a movie set.

"I thought you said it was messy," he said, joking as he filmed the view, then panned back to the apartment.

"Honestly, that was an excuse," she said, going into the kitchen.

"Sorry if I made you feel uncomfortable."

"Oh, it's not you, it's them," she said as she returned with a photo-quality flier in hand and gestured out the window to the mannequins below. "Now that we're here, alone, I feel much better," she said, her voice cold and distant.

Brayden looked at Marri and realized she was talking about the mannequins. That, and she had a letter opener in her other hand. "Heh, well enough to finish the interview?" he asked, trying to buy time as he glanced at the apartment door, which he noticed had numerous scratches marring its finish.

His heart raced as she spoke. "Sure," she said, handing him the flier. The front had a picture of The Hyperion with a bright yellow font, like a postcard, saying "Don't worry, we'll find you!" as if it were some kind of cheerful slogan. Brayden flipped it over to the back, where, in blood-red font, was the number 207.

The same number as this apartment building.

"The same number of people that lived in my hometown," she said. "You see, I've always felt uncomfortable around too many people, which you would think is a bad thing, except for what happens when I get too comfortable."

"What happens when you get too comfortable?" Brayden asked as he turned the camera towards her and took a half step back, pretending to get her into frame.

"I kill," she said, putting the sharp edge of the letter opener to the glass window and dragging it along its surface. The screech made Brayden wince. In that moment, she lunged, slashing the letter opener at him. Pain seared across his forearm as his blood splattered onto the floor. Instinct drove his back to the door and he yelled. One hand was on the doorknob as she lunged again, forcing him to roll to the side along the wall and run further into the apartment. Looking out, he could see all the mannequins were now out in the street, looking up into the apartment.

He reached for his gun as she swiped the letter opener across his midriff. Brayden jumped backward at the last second, avoiding disembowelment by a hair's breadth. She pulled down the shades as she neared him again, giving him enough time to draw his gun.

"Stop," he said, taking a shooting stance and pointing it at the center of her chest.

She stopped a half step away and eyed the gun, clearly gauging the space between them.

Brayden could feel her calculating her chances.

"Don't. Come into the apartment. I'll leave."

Without saying a word, she did as he said, giving Brayden room to leave. With his camera hand, he opened the door with just two fingers as pain shot up from his open wound. She followed him into the hallway until he was in sight of the mannequin, then her whole demeanor changed. No longer the dangerous cold animal, tears welled up in her eyes as he backed down the stairs.

"Please don't leave me here, Brayden.

"Please, I'll do anything.

"Please don't leave me with all these people."

Leaving the apartment, Brayden walked through the gauntlet of mannequins that had already moved to make a path for him. Looking up to the apartment, he saw the blinds were already closed, but was determined to keep his eyes there until he made it to the exit. To either side of him were mannequins of women, children, even babies, and he wondered for a grim moment just how she had killed all these people.

By the time he reached the exit and found it unlocked, Brayden had realized that they were her punishment, and that somehow in his visit to this apartment, he had gotten over his fear of mannequins.

With a sigh, he took to the stairs, climbing up to the third floor. From the landing, he could see the door for this floor. Heh, door number three. No one ever picked door number three on that old game show he used to watch with his grandma. He wondered why.

His musing was interrupted by a mocking whisper in his ear. Brayden felt his body erupt all at once in gooseflesh. He swallowed hard and tried to control his racing heart. Gulping air, he stopped to read a message scrawled onto the wall.

The Poet's Requiem
Tess P.

Gloating gates shriek
In discordant angst
To a ravaged cello's song.
Death hovers,
Breath bated
As alabaster fingers stroke frosted smiles
Upon slabs of silenced souls.
We know *our* worth, *our* place,
Need nothing more than a hell hole
For two debauched poets to drown
In stagnated syllables of despair.

Our grave trembles
Dug by depraved desires
Shared in dissolute dreams.
I whisper to the wraith by my side.
His warmth penetrates my pernicious soul
As our tongues twist in delicious damnation.

A wanton angel sways,
Weeping alone to a requiem,
The cello's final repose.

We raise wretched blades,
His to my nape,
Mine to his hallowed heart.

'On the count of three...'

3. Love Bomb, Baby
Alex Holmes

Traversing the dim hallway in search of whatever this level had to show him, Brayden stopped and turned quickly, hoping to catch a glimpse of whomever was following him. He kept hearing footsteps behind him, even the occasional sigh, but when he turned, he never caught so much as a heel or the corner of a garment, disappearing around a corner. Just... nothing. He had demanded and threatened, to no avail.

He caught himself before he stooped to pleading. *Let them follow*, he told himself. *It's probably standard for this place*, he reasoned. *I'm not going to fucking beg*, he concluded. Even so, by the time he found the door on the third floor, he was more than ready for some light, and more importantly, some distraction.

Brayden reached for the doorknob to enter, and found it locked. *Weird.* The first two, he'd just walked right in and started exploring. Irritated, he tried knocking.

"Who is there?" responded a woman's voice, promptly. Her accent was crisp and expensive-sounding. English, he thought. She sounded hot.

"I'm Brayden Winchell," he said, his voice dropping automatically into what he thought of as his ladies' man voice, a voice many women had learned to fear. He rubbed the notches on his belt absently. "I'm touring The Hyperion tonight, with permission from Management. I wondered if I could interview you."

"Do you have your invitation?" The door remained firmly closed.

"That postcard, you mean? No, I don't have it on me, but I have a scan I made to put on my channel. Will that work?"

"... I suppose. Hold it up to the peephole, please," the woman responded.

Brayden searched through his files on his phone and found the postcard. He enlarged the image to fill the screen and held it up to the peephole, as requested. He heard a series of locks being disengaged, and finally, the door opened to reveal a petite woman, probably in her early-30s, wearing a plain white shift. Her voice had not misled. She *was* hot. Super hot.

Brayden gave her a winning smile and held out his hand. "Brayden Winchell, as I said. Pleasure to meet you, Miss...?"

The woman looked down at his hand impassively. "Thank you, but I don't want to shake your hand."

"Fair enough," Brayden said, dropping his hand and adjusting his approach. "If I may come in, I'd love to hear–"

"Again, thank you, but no," the woman replied firmly. "I am obligated by contract to tell my story to any... *guest* of Management who wishes to hear it. I am not obligated to touch you or let you into my space. I will tell it from here."

She sat gracefully in the armchair that materialized at her back, not looking first to make sure it was there. Brayden had to admit – to himself – that it was a cool power move, even if he was annoyed by her multiple rejections.

"Is there another chair for me?" The question came out more petulantly than he'd intended, but he was done trying to impress this woman who still wouldn't tell him her name.

"There's one behind you," she replied.

Brayden thought there was a hint of mockery in her tone. *Bitch.* He didn't trust her enough to mimic her sitting without looking first, so he turned his head just enough to check that the chair was there – a twin to her armchair, except that where hers was white, to reflect the bright, minimalist décor of the room behind her, his was a deep wine red, to match the hallway he stood in. He sat and opened his camera. "Mind if I record this?"

The woman waved a hand and gave a curt nod of acceptance. "Very well. I will tell you my story. The story of how I came to be here. It starts with how I met my husband, John, and ends with – well, you'll see." She sat straight, arms on the chair, like a queen on her throne. She looked... somewhere else – not at Brayden, and her voice took on a far-off quality.

Lovebombing, they call it. I know that now. Fucking 'lovebombing'. There's no 'love' involved in lovebombing, believe me. But that's how we started, and – ultimately – that's how we got here, to The Hyperion. It's a shitty story, I know, but… well, aren't all the stories here, one way or another?

I don't even know when I first fell for John. He was the friend of a friend – Miles – a guy I'd been seeing who, as we soon worked out, shared the same interests, but no chemistry. We agreed we were much better off as mates than we were as a couple, and agreed to stay that way for our mutual best interests.

John was there, one night, at a party at Miles' house in Dalston, and we got to talking in the kitchen; yes, Jona Lewie was right, you can always find me in the kitchen at parties. Anyway, bored, I'd gone to get a refill, and there he was, stealing nibbles with one hand, a bottle of Pinot in the other, and sure, he was handsome and charming, and we got to chatting, but when my taxi arrived in the early hours of the morning, that, I thought, was that. As it turned out, John had other ideas.

He got my address off Miles, which I admit I was a bit pissed off about, but it seemed harmless enough at the time, so I just told him to please, kindly not give out my personal information to strangers in future, no matter how well *he* knew them, and left it at that. And it started nicely, if a little overwhelmingly – a delivery of cannoli from the patisserie I'd been raving about, with a little note saying, 'I thought you might need some sustenance after last night'. It was sweet, gentle.

Then, a couple of days later, it was flowers, nothing ostentatious, just a pretty summery bouquet and a card that said something like, 'I keep thinking about you', or words to that effect. It made me smile, after several months of dating disasters and swiping left.

I got his number off Miles, then, to say 'thank you'; it felt weird, oddly unsettling, this man sending me gifts without me having any way to contact him, so... I guess I was equally guilty of plying Miles for information.

Miles told me that John had some high-paying job in the city, single (yay!), travelled a lot for work, well-off, had been to the 'right' schools, yada yada. So, I messaged him, simply to say thanks, and we got chatting by text until we found ourselves exchanging messages later and later at night, maybe after a couple of glasses of wine, curled up on the sofa, and then, later still, in bed... and then the messages got more personal, more intimate, interspersed with compliments on the way I looked or what I'd been wearing the night we met– I never thought too much about the implications of that, at the time - a couple of late night phone calls, a delivery box of chocolates or wine here or there, and before I knew it, we'd been out for dinner a couple of times and I was waking up in his big, white-linened bed. So far, so good.

And the thing is, love's blind, right? Sure, I'd seen him lose his temper a few times, usually with waiters or theatre ushers, once with the guy in the garage who was meant to be fixing his car and had fucked up in some undisclosed but apparently catastrophic way, but he had a high-pressure job and he expected things to be done right. I never really thought that much of it.

He'd always been lovely to me, still charming, generous to a fault, showering me with gifts and

compliments aplenty. Everything seemed perfect
to this foolish girl, and I could finally stick two
fingers up at my mother and her 'you'll never find
a good man with your attitude,' and 'no man's
going to want a girl with tattoos on her thighs'
bullshit.

We were planning the wedding within six
months – stupid, I know, but I'll admit the
diamonds he placed on my finger over dinner in
the Seychelles blinded me a little, so of course, I
fucking said 'yes' – and married within twelve. It
was only once we were home from honeymoon
that I started to notice things I'd not seen before;
he was more aloof, stayed later at work, drank just
a glass of wine too many over dinner, the odd
whiskey before bed. His temper was looser, the
compliments fewer, interspersed with snide
comments here and there about my weight –
which, incidentally, had never changed – my
clothes, my hair. You know the sort of thing.

Gradually, they became more the norm;
putting me down in front of our friends – whom
he, of course, distanced me from, finding fault
with each – telling me that things I'd said were
stupid, gaslighting about things he'd said or done
that he subsequently claimed had never happened.
He took control of the money, after a while, giving
me 'an allowance' for clothes and hairdressers and
the like, because – as he put it – 'I earn most of it,
baby, you don't make a regular income from your
little paintings, so this way you've always got
money in the bank when you need something'.

It made sense, or it seemed to, and I went
along with it; he was right, the income from sales
of my art – sculptures, as well as paintings – was
good, when it came, but sporadic. I could sell three

pieces through the Highgate gallery in a week and then have nothing for months. It did – almost – make financial sense. He paid the mortgage on the house anyway, all the bills, so... sure. Why not? I was a kept woman, and as much as my latent feminism blinked a warning eye at the back of my mind every so often, I'll admit a large part of me liked that. I never saw it as controlling, at the time.

The first time he hit me was a shock, I won't lie. I never believed 'dumbstruck' was actually a physical thing, but there we have it. And of course – predictably enough – he was wracked with remorse and the inevitable self-pity afterwards; 'it'll never happen again, Clo, I've never been sorrier for anything in my life, please don't leave me, I love you, I'm nothing without you'. You know the routine.

It did happen again, of course, harder, and predictably, more frequently and more purposeful each time, and each time it destroyed my resistance just that little bit more. I thought about leaving, of course I did, but where would I go? Mother and I seldom spoke anyway, less so since he'd cut those ties for me by calling her a barren old cunt at New Year's. My friends had all drifted away over time as he'd built the walls around me higher and higher – imperceptible, but there all the same - until one day everyone apart from him was on the outside. I had no money of my own, no regular income, I'd given up my flat; even my car was in John's name.

So I did what all of us do; I cried silently in the shower behind the locked bathroom door, then pulled on my big-girl knickers, painted on a brave face, and got on with trying to be as invisible as possible when he was in one of 'those' moods. We all know how to do it, those of us who've been there, just sort of fading into semi-translucence and trying not to say anything contentious while still being attentive and present enough that we can't be accused of ignoring them. I lay awake some nights, when he'd drunk too much, breathing quietly and praying he'd fall asleep quickly before the otherwise inevitable pawing and spittle-lubed penetration and comments about my being a frigid bitch could start, and I dreamed about somehow magically getting away.

And that's where this all comes about. Magic. That's, ultimately, why I'm here. Any fool can grab for a kitchen knife in the midst of self-defence, sure, but who was going to believe that? John was always very careful that the marks were hidden, after all, and my shame and self-reproach were great enough that I couldn't have told anyone the truth even if I'd had people left to tell. No, this – I thought – was much better.

I'd never considered myself 'a witch'. I mean, who does? But that's what I am, I suppose, or was. When Grandma – it's always the grandmother, isn't it? – used to talk to me about 'the craft' when I was young, or make those little admonishments about how 'dolls have power' or how 'words are important', I never really paid much heed. My mother used to get angry with her 'folklore nonsense', but then Mother got angry about a lot of things, and I just thought Grandma was a fun old lady who enjoyed entertaining her only grandchild with spooky stories. Halloween was always Samhain in Marjorie's house, and there were always candles and the faint smell of sage in the woodsmoke of the old fireplace, but even Mother used to think that was just the idiosyncrasies of growing up 'country'. It wasn't until Grandma died, four years into my marriage to John, that I started to think differently.

I didn't go to the funeral; John had seen to that already, so I only found out she'd passed on through a rather terse and formal letter from Mother and her new husband, who'd clearly still not got over the 'barren' comment from a couple of years previously. I didn't go to the will-reading, either – why would I? – so it was a surprise when, a couple of weeks later, a box arrived via courier.

It makes sense, I suppose – why would she leave any of it to Mother, when she disliked her daughter as much as my mother disliked her, and my mother had clearly never believed an iota of it anyway. Even so, I took the parcel and hid it away at the back of the hall closet, not daring to open it until a couple of weeks later when John was overseas on yet another business trip.

I found out later – again, how predictable in hindsight – that most of these 'business trips' had names; Charlotte, Sophie, the ever-so-exotic Monique, in France. That's not why I did what I did, though, let's be clear about that. I felt many emotions about John by this point, but jealousy was definitely not one of them. If he was spending his time fawning and fucking with some side-piece or other, it meant he was less likely to expect me to dutifully open my legs for him, and had less opportunity to dig an elbow into my stomach or make my teeth rattle with another slap.

No, this was self-preservation mixed, I admit, with a smattering of revenge, but it had nothing to do with the other women. I just hope he didn't treat any of them how he treated me. I can't feel

anything other than pity for them and the lies he
must have told them.

Anyway. The box. You can imagine – a bunch
of assorted paraphernalia, half-burned candles
and pestles and mortars and the like, and a bunch
of photographs of my great- and great-great
grandparents. All the usual detritus of a life that
one day was meaningful and the next was just…
stuff. One photograph, framed, tattered and lightly
colour-faded, was still clearly me as a child,
Mother, and Grandma – the Mother, the Maiden,
and the Crone, right? How clichéd.

But in amongst the mildly-goth décor and
circus-side-tent accoutrements were two very old,
very hand-written books, and a collection of jars,
bottles, and unusual-scented lotions. It's amazing,
opening a couple of those, just how evocative of
time and place scent can be. Memory-triggering.
That's one thing we miss, here: Smells, other than
the occasional whiff of sulphur, I guess. Opening
that box, I was transported straight back to
Grandma's parlour, the cupboard at the back
where we weren't supposed to go, but which was,
therefore, the perfect hide-and-seek winner every
time.

It's funny, to those who think of witchery as
the fictional warty old hag living in a cottage in the
forest, flying on broomsticks and cackling over a
bubbling cauldron, just how much of the craft is
actually just basically hedge-science, or chemistry,
or simple herbalism or first aid.

Those old women – who, in reality, weren't
actually that old, other than the world-weariness
that a hard lifetime of scratching out a living with a
vegetable patch and a couple of chickens, and the

occasional beneficence of townsfolk she helped
with some midwifery or a herbal poultice or
something – were ostracised, a lot of the time,
close to the community, but not part of it, at least
until someone wanted something. And then the
constant knowledge that you needed to be on your
game at all times, 'cos if old Jeremiah's cow got
sick or little Jacob caught a fever, you were liable
to get the blame for it if you weren't careful. It
must have been exhausting; no wonder they all
looked old before their time.

Anyway, that's where we came in, really; those
old books, filled with scratchy inkblot handwriting
about potions for this and concoctions for that,
drawings and diagrams of plants and body-parts
alike. I learned, later, that they were grimoires,
handbooks of practice and ritual, recipes – if you
can call them that – and charms, the use of plants,
incantations, and scrying by bones or leaves,
handed down from mother to daughter, jealously
guarded, yet shared with like-minded practitioners
when required.

Some of it, I immediately dismissed as
superstitious nonsense – I was a modern twenty-
first century woman with a smartphone and an
espresso machine. No way was I heading off to the
crossroads at midnight to have sex with the Devil,
I had quite enough of that at home – but the
herbalism, initially, seemed to call to me. And I do
mean 'call to me'. Repeatedly. Over and over, like
an earworm of a song you just can't get out of your
head.

I'd initially put everything back in the box,
pushed to the back of the cupboard knowing that
John would never find it behind the cleaning
products and bin-liners there wasn't a cat in hell's

chance of him ever touching. That, as he told me repeatedly, was women's work; he earned the money, I looked after the home. Who would have guessed that a man with such outward charm could be such a misogynistic prick at heart? But that night – and for several nights after – I dreamed of the books, pages rippling like some living things, over and over, the same dream night after night.

I'd no real choice but to wait until John took an overnight in Edinburgh (who I later learned was called Katy. With a 'y'.) before digging the mottled leather journals back out of their resting place and carrying them to the bleached wood island in the kitchen. And as if by magic – which, of course, it was – there they were, those pages, exactly as I'd dreamed about. How could that be? I'd literally flicked through them, glancing at bits here and there, but certainly not with enough attentiveness to retain that level of detail.

Was it my subconscious mind trying to nudge me toward a solution, or something more... enchanting, Marjorie's hand guiding me from beyond the veil? Now, if you'd said that to me at the time, I'd have laughed in your face – I'd never been a believer, never one for tales of ghostly interventions or Heaven and Hell, and yet here we are. Just goes to show how much I knew, right?

If it was Gran, she certainly knew where to start; like I said, I wasn't suddenly going to strip naked and dance with the Devil in the pale moonlight, but herbs and traditional medicines? That was basically science; everyone knew that Aspirin originally came from willow bark and that Witch Hazel was an anti-inflammatory, right? And that's where the idea first started. It wasn't a plot to bump him off, I swear it wasn't, not at the outset anyway.

It was more self-preservation than that; I figured that, if he was low-level ill and mildly debilitated, he'd be marginally less likely to hold me under an icy shower for twenty minutes or hurl the dinner across the table in a cold fury because he'd hedged wrongly at work and lost some client a chunk of imaginary money in ones and zeroes on a spreadsheet. And there it was, two tiny brown glass bottles of Buckthorn Bark and Milk Thistle. Nothing serious, nothing life-threatening or irreversible; just some minor abdominal discomfort, nausea, and the shits. Perfect.

John was more than used to me eating differently to him anyway, especially at breakfast time; he'd pour out some hearty bowl of granola with oat milk, while I was more often than not likely to go with a couple of slices of Honeydew and a coffee. So it was easy. I didn't need to use much, the tiniest amounts really, and it's frighteningly easy to secrete bark shavings in with cereal that looks like fucking woodchips anyway, and so that was that.

By that first evening, he was complaining of stomach cramps, and after a couple of weeks of no let-up in his symptoms (well, of course, there weren't, I'd mixed the bark shavings in through the entire box, and the next one too) and a trip to some private Harley Street consultant, he was diagnosed with IBS brought on by stress.

It turns out, of course, that Grandma was right; I *did* have an aptitude for this stuff, just like she'd always said she could see in me when I was young. Adding in a little Valerian Root and Sweet

Flag every so often mixed up the nausea and added an occasional cracking headache that sent him off to bed with a stupid eye-mask, complaining of photosensitivity and heart palpitations (surprise, surprise), exacerbated on occasion by the liberal addition of Yohimbe and Saw Palmetto in with the T2 chai blend I 'thoughtfully' bought him to help him 'relax'. The poor man just didn't seem to be able to get any respite from his ailments, no matter what that expensive doctor prescribed, and no-one – apart, of course, from me – had the faintest idea what was behind it all.

I'd have been content with his failing, but definitely non-terminal, health decline, I promise I would, if he hadn't come back from one of his 'business trips' more violent and hate-filled than usual. It turns out that the lover of the moment had seen through his web of fictions and told him in no uncertain terms to do one and never darken her adulterous doorstep again, and of course – as far as John was concerned – I was to blame for that.

That was an unpleasant evening; the first time I'd been genuinely concerned that the 'punishment' might not stop while I was still breathing. I don't know if you've ever been repeatedly choked until you almost pass out. I can categorically state that it's not fun. With just enough time between to force enough air into your screaming lungs to keep awake, knowing that it's going to start all over again any second, whiskey-fumes breathed into your face from close-range and covered in your own drool and tears; no. Not one for the faint-hearted.

It was the first time John had left 'public' bruises, too, giving rise to a week or so of almost constant silk scarf camouflage. It took that long for my voice to return to normal, too, and for a couple of days, I was genuinely concerned that he might have done some actual permanent damage to my larynx. I determined that that would never be happening again; something more than herbalism was required.

I was exhausted; emotionally and physically, and that, I suppose, led me to the idea. Either that or, once again, the idea led me to itself, like a Siren on the rocks. Toward the back of one of the grimoires was what I felt I needed; something that would make John too worn-out to take his shit out on me for a while. It was tougher than just sneaking herbs into his food, and I had to plan my timing much more carefully, waiting until the following weekend when I knew he was out of town again.

It also meant that I had to set-aside my 'age of technology' scepticism and trust in the power of Grandma, and I won't lie when I say that I felt fucking self-conscious as I sat on the lounge floor in a white shift-dress with lighted candles at the four cardinal points, trying to make sense of the fatigue curse scratched into the old paper.

But, like I said, I had an unexpected aptitude for this, and low and behold, John returned from his trip two days early, citing crushing exhaustion and general malaise. I'd be lying if I said I wasn't delighted and not a little proud of myself, especially when the fatigue didn't shift after a reasonable 'getting over jet-lag' period and it became apparent that something more serious was going on.

The Harley Street guy thought it might be related to the gastrointestinal upset, something about the ongoing diarrhoea causing difficulty in absorbing nutrients and vitamins, or possibly to the underlying stress itself, and... well. Who was I to argue with medicine's finest and most expensive? It had the added benefit of giving John some – by the sound of it – fairly terrifying nightmares at times, too, meaning that despite earlier and earlier bed-times – leaving me greater time in safety on my own downstairs – he spent much of the night whimpering and twitching and arose for work the following morning less refreshed and more sallow and exhausted than ever. Job done. Or it would have been, had I not fucked up.

You see, the thing I hadn't taken into consideration was the effect the lack of sleep and the general feeling of shitty health would have on John's already loosening temper. Now, don't for a moment think I'm excusing his behaviour here, I'm not; we all know people who get ratty when they're tired or hungry, but they don't all manifest that by knocking seven shades of shit out of their nearest and supposedly dearest. But it *was*, I'll admit, a strategic miscalculation on my part, which was evidenced a few weeks later when John decided he'd had enough one day at the office, and took the tube home early to rest.

Of course, as Sod's Law would have it, this would be the one time I'd decided not to spend the day scrubbing bathrooms or batch-cooking or any one of the dozen or so other tasks which we could easily have afforded someone to come in and do were John not so determined to keep me very much to myself in the house, instead retiring to the spare bedroom with a rare afternoon glass of wine and my sketchbook.

John arrived home and – despite me still nominally at least being a professional artist and selling works through the gallery – announced that I was 'nothing but a freeloading, lazy, worthless little whore', swanning around living the life of Riley like some libertine dandy while he 'flogged himself to exhaustion and an early grave' to earn the money to keep us both. The headaches, nightmares, and general fatigue had clearly got the better of him – my fault, yes – what was left of his temper finally collapsed into rubble, and thus began the worst night of my life.

Firstly, the sketchbooks – six months' worth of painstaking work towards a particular commission, including the original subject photographs – went onto the log burner, to curl and ultimately vanish into ash, while John dragged me across to watch by the hair, hauling me over the lounge floor by the scalp; then my brushes, pencils, and charcoals were all snapped – hundreds of pounds worth of art supplies from my 'allowance' – and thrown into the fire as well, before he turned his attention from my art box and, instead, onto me directly.

The slaps and the kidney punches were bad enough, and it took a week until I stopped peeing blood, but it was the cruelty of John's coup de grace that destroyed me; deliberately, despite my sobbing and pleading, using his superior weight and strength to straddle my supine body on the lounge rug, he proceeded to systematically dislocate each of my fingers and thumbs at the knuckle. Slowly, one at a time, as I begged. *Crack. Crack. Crack*, like sticks snapping, each one punctuated by another insult. 'Cunt'. 'Whore'. 'Slut', before eventually – thankfully - storming out once more and leaving me sobbing and broken, foetal, in the corner.

Now, I accept, this would be the point that I should have simply packed up my stuff and run for the nearest Police station; not I, though. I can't describe to you the pain of self-relocating those fingers one at a time, biting down on the broken shaft of a paintbrush to subdue my screams, but that pain clarified both my thinking and my purpose.

Two days later, while he was off somewhere once more, I worked the wax of one of Grandma's votive candles into a vaguely human shape, pressing some of the loose hair from John's hairbrush and nail-clippings from his bathroom wastebasket into the centre and working through the charms and invocations from the back of the book, blessing the poppet and naming it for him.

People assume that the 'like creates like' of sympathetic fetish magic works exactly like that; stick a pin in somewhere, and the target suddenly and instantly experiences crushing, unbearable pain in the corresponding spot. It doesn't. But, as my fingers healed – albeit with some stiffness and residual aching in cold weather – over the next few months, John's already failing health suddenly fell off a cliff; a series of maladies, all untreatable by modern medicine, but clearly symptomatic, hospital visits and scans and blood-tests, before he finally succumbed to what his doctors eventually described as idiopathic degenerative multi-organ failure in a private Knightsbridge HIV clinic, 'idiopathic' apparently being clever doctor-speak for 'we haven't got a bloody clue'. Poor man.

By the end, I almost felt sorry for him. Not enough to stop pushing hat pins into the rapidly deteriorating wax, obviously, but almost.

So, finally, I was free of him, revenge being a dish best served significantly chilled, and without any of that messy arrest and court appearance stuff that would have come with the kitchen-knife approach, complete with the full grieving-widow schtick and a very tidy pay-out, thank you very much, from his pension and life-insurance policies following his tragic and inexplicably terminal illness. And for the next four years, that seemed to be the end of it. I'd got away with it, without any of those cartoon 'meddling kids' or Columbo-esque 'one more thing's; good old Grandma. But this, it seems, is where I made my fatal miscalculation.

No-one, I'm sure you'll agree, would have blamed me for seeking my own kind of way out of the torment I'd found myself in, and probably – had I taken the 'kitchen knife' solution – most courts and juries would have been sympathetic anyway, after a suitably traumatic soul-bearing and a few months on remand. But it was the method, rather than the outcome, that was my downfall. Apparently, you see, the use of witchcraft for maleficent purposes allowed no grey areas; using the craft to harm another human, no matter how much they objectively deserved it, went against nature and, it seemed, against the laws of God. It was, make no mistake, an irredeemable sin, and there's only one place that sinners like that get sent; the down elevator.

That was a part that wasn't in Grandma's book; the apparent contract between the practitioner and the Devil himself. And the Devil, it seems, has a sense of humour and his own timetable, which explains the early-hours of the morning visitation I received from a delegation of Hell's own demonic council, explaining to me exactly what the eternal price I was expected to pay for my transgression was, and which led – ultimately – to my terrified pre-dawn flight to St. Michael's Church in Highgate, screaming for priests and salvation and wittering incomprehensibly about fire and brimstone and fiends and their associated hellhounds.

I don't blame them for sectioning me, that night, on an emergency observational hold; I would have, too, if I'd seen me tearing through the streets in my nightwear, hair dishevelled and wild-eyed and petrified, and to all intents and purposes in the midst of a full-on schizophrenic breakdown presumably – as far as the duty psychiatrist was concerned – finally brought about by the awful, unexpected death of my soul-mate husband and my subsequent loneliness and withdrawal.

They put me down as a suicide, two days later, and again I couldn't blame them, even as I catatonically watched the bedsheets coil themselves into that makeshift noose. After all, what other explanation could there be? The ultimate 'locked-room mystery', a secure hospital room with no access for anyone save the nurses and medical staff? Everyone knows that magic and witchcraft don't exist in a rational, modern worldview, and who could be that surprised that the quiet woman from number 23 finally felt her mind crack apart through paranoid depression and so took the only way out left to her?

Except we know better, don't we? Which is why, ultimately, we're here, for eternity, in The

Hyperion. Damnation, it seems, has a way of being inescapable, no matter what.

Brayden sat, spellbound, for long seconds after she stopped speaking. It wasn't until she stood, abruptly, and began to close the door, that he turned his camera off and stood, as well, trying to think of something to say. "Wait," he said, somewhat desperately, before the door hid her from view. "I have questions!"

The woman regarded him coldly. "I am required to participate in the Orientation by telling you how I came to be here," she said flatly. Her eyes dropped to where he fingered the notches on his belt, and one corner of her mouth lifted slightly. "Enjoy your stay."

Brayden could only stand, dumb, and listen to the many locks sliding back into place. He looked back down the hall toward the stairs. Time to go up one more.

He was brought up short at the top of the stairs by the sight of a figure, the first he had encountered in these damned hallways. He could tell from the landing that something was not right with her.

She was filthy, to begin with, her dark hair matted and unkempt. The high-necked gray nightgown she wore was stained and torn. Thin bare legs and feet jutting out from the bottom were caked with dirt. Her nails were long and ragged, the color of parchment.

Nearing, Brayden watched in horrified fascination as she smeared a festering wound on one arm across the wall, next to lines she had written in a similar medium already, before using a finger from the opposite hand to continue writing. He paused behind her to read, but immediately, she stopped writing, tilting her head to sniff the air, as if only then detecting his presence.

Her head swiveled around impossibly far, the movement more owl than human, until Brayden could see her ravaged face, from her bared teeth, broken and yellow, to the sunken eye sockets sewn shut with stout red thread. He backed away slowly.

Phantom
C.E. Wallace

Wandering
through rows of
      crumbling stone
my thoughts
buried deep
    as bones
      beneath my feet

Hearing echoes
    of the past
in the way the
    wind whistles
    through the grave

perhaps
the monster that lurks
here is not what they
        say
not one born of
fur and fang but
        the one that's
        born of grief

the most terrifying
        specter of them all
is the one you
                cannot
                        see

4. Time to Wake Up and Smell the Coffee

Andrew Harrowell

Brayden dashed up the stairs to the next level of the building, putting as much distance between him and the warped words on the wall as he could. The dark poem pushed its way into his mind, but he fought against it. He wasn't going to look back. He wasn't going to give whoever had scrawled the craziness the satisfaction. He kept his attention forward. He was going to get through this bizarre haunted house, if it was the last thing he did.

It better not be.

He dismissed the thought, as his eyes took in a single door down the dimly-lit hallway. Paint peeled away from the shabby wooden frame. As he watched, a little metal number four suddenly gave up its own survival efforts and fell from the structure. Brayden glared down at it.

"I'm better than this place," he told the empty passage, his eyes exploring the darkness. There was no alternative entrance or exit on this level. Brayden shrugged, placed his hand on the dull doorknob, and drew a breath. He told himself he was going to show the building who was boss. And when he did, his followers would delight in the tale. This story was going viral.

He might even be looking at product endorsements. That's how hard he was going to kick this building's arse.

Brayden's back straightened, his head lifted. He turned the door handle and stepped into something that wasn't an apartment. It was more like a one-level house. A tiny kitchenette sat to his left; a dining table had been positioned just ahead of him. Even with the little he could make out, Brayden felt like the place had been plucked out of some Good Housekeeping magazine from the 1960s or 70s. The only thing missing was the professional lighting. His eyes held on the kitchen window. There was nothing but blackness beyond it.

"Thank goodness, you're here!" A thin face pushed in front of Brayden's vision and he flinched. "It's about time." Greased back hair didn't move as the head bobbed away. Red braces hung over slim shoulders, the off-white vest half-tucked into brown pants.

"What are you talking about?" Brayden demanded, watching the man move into the kitchen, his hand coming to rest on the handle of a bubbling percolator. A bitter smell stung Brayden's nostrils and he wrinkled his nose.

"You understand. You get it. That's why I need your support." Black liquid sloshed this way and that as the man's hand swung the coffee pot wildly around. "You know that The Hyperion is going to make me rich."

Brayden's brow creased. He eyed the character before him. He looked like the only TikTok he understood was the one coming from a clock. But could that just be an act? Brayden tried to keep his tone even.

"How is this freak show going to make you money?"

"Isn't it obvious?" The man's eyes shone as he advanced. There was a soft spatter as coffee spilt onto the floor. "Books, tours. Imagine me as a guest lecturer from East to West Coast. I will be able to demand any fee I like, once I've been through that building."

"But you're in The Hyperion." Brayden scowled.

"Pffff," the man raspberried. "Once I'm on that Greyhound, I'll be in Chicago in good time for its appearance."

"No, you don't understand." Ire rose in Brayden's throat. "Today is Halloween. The Hyperion is here."

The man twisted away and explored the kitchen for a mug. There was none on the side, and a few bangs of the cupboard revealed empty shelves. He turned back to Brayden and chugged the coffee straight from the pot. With a smack of his lips, he continued, "You really aren't with it today, are you?" Quickly, he crossed the short distance. A rough hand landed on Brayden's shoulder, the face leering forward. Brayden's fingers found the baton in his pocket.

"Get off me." He shrugged himself away from the wide eyes. "You are crazy."

The man's hands went high, then the pot crashed to the counter with force. He twirled on his heel and stalked across the space, arms gesturing upwards, unspoken words coming to his dark lips. Braydon inched forward, his hand still clenched around his weapon, mind full of uncertainty. The man paused next to a low-level sideboard, his fingers caressing the speaker of a dusty record player.

"I'll only be mad if I miss this chance." He swung round, pacing straight at Brayden, his eyes growing wider. His balled-up fist landed on his outstretched palm, as he ground to a halt. "If I'm not on that bus this evening, I won't forgive myself. Everything I've worked for. All the effort I've put in. It will be wasted. I'm so close now, so very near to making my fame and fortune. I just need to make it onto that bus."

Brayden's eyes rolled upwards. He was almost ready to seek divine intervention. When he spoke, his voice was low.

"You need to listen to me. It is October 31st! You are in The Hyperion, but this place is messed up…"

"Nonsense." The figure started stalking back towards the record collection. "Stop having fun with old Harry. I don't have time for your games."

Brayden launched forward, rounding the table, and snagged Harry with his free hand. He pulled him close, the smell of stale cigarettes clogging his nose.

"This is serious."

"Exactly." The whites of Harry's eyes were as large as dinner plates. The tiny pupils stayed fixed on Brayden for a long moment. Harry blinked. Brayden shifted away.

"What is wrong with you?"

"Me?" Arms went wide and Harry puffed out his chest. "Why aren't you helping me? I need you to get me out of here."

Brayden breathed a sigh of relief.

"Finally, you are talking sense." He glanced over his shoulder towards the door he'd entered by. Thinking back to what was below, he shuddered. "I don't think we can go down. There's..." He sucked a deep breath, returned his attention to the other man. "Well, let's just say you don't want to go that way."

"Down?"

"Yeah, the lower floors." In response to Harry's look, Brayden ploughed on, "Maybe things have changed since you arrived, but trust me, steer clear. I reckon we should go up. How do we get off this level?" He glanced into the gloom, trying to spot a way out. Harry was suddenly at his side, his knuckles lightly rapping on Brayden's forehead.

"Hello? We go out the door, get in your car and you take me to the bus station. Unless, of course, you want to drive me all the way to Chicago. Waste of a ticket, but I'd enjoy it more. We can catch up. Talk about the good days." His lips curled up. "Plan what I'm going to do with all my riches."

"What are you talking about? I don't know you!" Brayden took a step back and bumped into the table. He composed himself, ready for the speech he felt he needed to give. The words that would feature so prominently in the tale he'd tell when he got out of here. "But together we can make it out of this. You and..."

"Don't you start. You're meant to have my back!"

"I do." Brayden snagged the man's flailing wrist. "You and me together. We can make it to safety..."

"Safety?" Harry wrenched away, his hands flying up to the side of his head. White fingers spiked out his hair as they dragged away. "How are you not getting this? I'm getting myself in harm's way, and it will be the making of me."

Brayden wiped his hand down his face. Exasperated, his voice hitched up, "Too late! You are in here already. Why won't you listen to me?"

"Because he's not really here." A voice welled up from behind Harry's shoulder. Brayden shoved the man aside and took in the frail woman on the couch. Her hands curled tightly together in the lap of her long, blue dress. Dim emerald eyes twinkled from beneath deep forehead furrows.

"I'm not listening because you are as bad as her." Harry appeared at Brayden's side. The slap on his arm was heavy, but filled with warmth. "You are meant to be getting me out of here. Or at least trying to help me change her mind."

"Wait..." Brayden's attention flicked from one to the other. His jaw loosened.

"No, there's no time to waste." Harry's head bobbed up and down as he spoke. "I need to pack. You deal with her for me." He dismissed the woman and moved towards the far end of the room. In the gloominess, Brayden could just make out two doorways. A light flicked on through one and Brayden saw a shabby suitcase land on the corner of a bed.

"We shall have some time now. He spends an average of twelve to fourteen minutes trying to pack."

Brayden held the figure's stare for a long moment before clarity welled up within him.

"It's you that entered, isn't it?"

"You're smart, dear. Although not that bright." Her eyes took in the dull yellow walls around her. They caught on a drinks trolley against the wall, and her tongue flicked across dry lips.

"But where are my manners? May I offer you a drink?"

She eased to her feet, and Brayden cringed as he heard something click.

"Who are you?"

"You will forgive me. It's been a while since I have had guests...or maybe it hasn't. Either way, my name remains Diane Morris. Coffee?"

Slowly, she shuffled towards the kitchen space. Her foot snagged on the linoleum and she stumbled. Brayden pounced and snatched at her outfit. There was very little of her underneath the garment.

"You okay?" He steadied the woman and she smiled sweetly at him. Something in Diane's face stirred his emotions.

"Fine, thank you."

Brayden rubbed at his chin, the prickles of his stubble jarring him. How long had he been here already?

Too long. Time to do something impressive. Find out what you need. Get out of here. Be smart, for once.

He flicked a glance at the other lit room. It looked like a drawer had been emptied into the suitcase.

"What about him? He seems a lot younger than you."

Rather than turning towards Harry, who continued to crash around the bedroom, Diane focused on the man before her.

"A figment of the past. A testament to what I used to be."

Brayden eyes roamed the grimy décor.

"Nineteen sixty-one." The pair shared a look, the unasked question hanging between them.

Brayden did the maths and whistled. "Don't. Please." Her eyes held a tired sadness. "I don't think I can stand to know."

Diane released herself from Brayden's grip and wobbled to the kitchen counter. She stared into the sink, a small avalanche of dishes facing her. Scooping up the cleanest mug she could spot, she ran her wrinkled fingers around the rim, then drew together cracked lips to blow at it.

Satisfied with her efforts, she turned to the counter and clutched at the half-full pot. It rose slightly and then sagged.

"Here, let me." Brayden moved around her and poured the drink. "Do you want me to clean up a little?"

"Why bother?" Diane wrapped her hands around the mug, savouring the warmth. "They will be there tomorrow. Or whatever the difference between now and the next time I make it here is. Shall I pour you a cup? It will help. Trust me."

Brayden rubbed at his lips. How long had it been since he'd last had a drink? Was coffee what he needed? His eyes caught on the drinks trolley. "Really, dear?" Diane asked at his side. "I mean, are you even old enough to drink?" She gave Brayden a half smile, and then flicked her wrist. "Be my guest."

The moment was gone, and he turned back to his host.

"What happened? How did you get here?"

"Probably the same as you." Diane shuffled across the floor, pausing at the couch. "It's alluring, isn't it? Once the letters start."

Brayden thought back to the texts he'd received. They couldn't have been the same. Not in the sixties. "For me, it was almost like having an affair." Diane glanced towards the bedroom.

"For once, I felt like I was living his life. Having secrets, sneaking around."

"Don't you ever quit?" Harry demanded as he marched into the room, socks dangling from both his hands. "Nag, nag, nag. Just can it!" He glared at an empty spot on the carpet, before he disappeared back into the bedroom.

"Well, that answers why you did it," Brayden
deadpanned.

Diane huffed at him, as she slumped down,
wincing as the chair's thin material wheezed
underneath her.

"Tell me, do you have someone waiting for you
on the outside?"

Brayden's mind twitched, as possibilities raced
across his mind. Jessica had been his latest
conquest. Sure, he'd told her he wanted to see her
again, but only on the chance he might be in need
of some 'companionship'. Or if he couldn't score
someone better. It would be hard to find someone
fitter than her.

No, Jessica wouldn't be worried about him.

There were his parents. Not his father. He
wouldn't be concerned. But Mom would. Probably
not worrying yet. How long would it take? If he
wasn't home tomorrow, she'd accept that.

The day after? The next? Whenever it was,
she'd start asking questions. Sending Dad out to
check his usual haunts. Brayden shivered, then
focused himself on the seated woman.

"I do ma'am," he told Diane, shifting his eyes
away from the questioning stare.

"You know I'm not that much older than you."

That brought Brayden's head around, but
Harry broke his concentration.

"Are these clean?" He wagged a pair of pants
at the room, before hollering, "Well, how am I
supposed to know?" Harry stomped away, as
Diane tutted and muttered,

"Oh dear. That's unfortunate."

Brayden turned to her and immediately averted his eyes. "Not to worry. They will smell for a while, then all will be fine." Brayden tried not to listen to the sound of the withered hand scraping across the top of the dress.

"Can I...errrr...get you anything?" He had found a viewless window to stare out.

"It's fine," came the curt reply as Diane rose again. "Refill? Oh wait, you didn't have one, did you? Let me pour."

"Where's my good shirt?" Harry screamed.

"In your damn wardrobe, where's it been every other time you asked!" Diane screeched back.

Brayden watched the woman slowly rise and step towards the kitchen. His heart was heavy. Diane had been here for more than seventy years, cut off from her family, her loved ones.

"You don't deserve this."

"Oh." Her eyes were bright as she took him in. "Harry isn't – wasn't – all that bad. Even if it feels like it when you are stuck with the worst moment of his life, over and over."

"It seems like he was intent on getting here. How come you did it and not him?"

"Does it matter? After all this time, I know what I did. I know why I must be here."

Brayden moved closer, laying his hand on her arm and squeezing.

"How about we get you out of here?"

"I don't think you understand. I've had a long time to think. This is my punishment."

Brayden pulled her closer to him. She stank of sour milk, the legacy, perhaps, of the stains on her dress.

"You weren't to know. You said it yourself, this place is exciting. Once you're in contact, it's hard to keep away. It kind of takes over your mind." He saw it now.

"Well, that's nice to know. Like him, were you?" She shifted her head in the direction of the bedroom. "An adventurer. Did you think this place would be the making of you?"

Brayden didn't want to answer. He suddenly felt self-conscious. He slipped past the woman, examining what he could see. The two doorways lay ahead. The shadow of Harry waving clothing around stretched long across the wall through one.

"There has to be a way to get out."

"Coffee, dear?"

A steaming cup of brown liquid appeared before Brayden. "It will make everything better, easier."

A crooked smile twisted the woman's face, as she pushed the filthy mug towards him.

Brayden couldn't help but think of his mom. She was always on hand with a hot drink whenever times were tough. He stared at the leering face, and dismissed the sense of familiarity.

This isn't real, he told himself. "Yes, it is." Diane's wispy eyebrows arched up, and she cackled. "It's all you've got now. Have your coffee, and sit. The four of us can make it work."

"Why the hell aren't my brown shoes where I left them?" Harry fussed into the room, dipped his head below the couch, before he whirled and headed into the kitchen.

Brayden watched him go, as his mind ticked over the problem. There was no obvious escape.

But someone was talking to him. Diane understood the situation, and she had been here years.

Maybe Harry could be broken out of this...loop, or whatever it was.

They could beat this place.

Diane. Him. Harry. All three of them.

Three.

"You said four." He stared at the woman. "What did you mean four?"

"Well," a mischievous look brightened her face. "I couldn't leave her with him, could I? Not after what I did."

Brayden stepped back. His hand found his baton again and closed around it.

"You brought a kid in here? Here!" His mind recalled the sour-smelling stain on Diane's dress, and he just stopped himself throwing up.

"Coffee?"

He slapped the cup away.

"You monster," he seethed. "How could you do that to a child? Your own flesh and blood?"

Diane stared ahead, her eyes focused on nothing.

"I wasn't to know, was I? I couldn't have foreseen this. Besides, she couldn't stay with her father."

Brayden's tone was low, his words barely above a whisper.

"Where is she?"

"Don't worry yourself. I've put her to sleep."

Immediately, Brayden was running towards the dark doorway. He pushed into the small space, and hurried to the cot. There, swaddled in a soft pink blanket, lay a very blue little child. Brayden grabbed at the bundle and rushed back.

"Quick," he implored Diane, as he cuddled the child to his chest. She was so cold, so horribly still. "Tell me what you did. Maybe I can help. Medicine, it's come so far since...since..."

Diane waved him off.

"Nonsense, young man. She will be fine soon. It's not long and we can do it all over again. Now, have a drink."

"Yes, do." Harry stood by the kitchen, coffee pot loosely held in his hand. Blood poured down his chin. "The coffee's excellent." Drops of red sprayed from his mouth as he wobbled and slumped to his knees. Then he crashed face-first onto the ground.

"What...why?" Brayden's attention snapped from the dead man to the lifeless bundle at his chest. Then he found the eyes of Diane. They were empty, lost.

Darkness closed around them. Brayden shifted round. No longer could he see Harry, nor the kitchen. He shifted back, and he could barely spot Diane against the darkness that was closing in. The dead child in his arms seemed lighter. He tried to pull her closer, but she was gone.

Blackness surrounded Brayden, and then a light snapped on.

A single door sat in the centre of the darkened space. The glare gleamed off its perfect white surface. Brayden didn't know what was ahead of him, what was to come next. But he knew he wasn't staying here a second longer.

He ran. Not just from what he had seen, the tragedy of the last few minutes. But he also desperately wanted to get back to what he had left behind.

He pushed through the door without another thought.

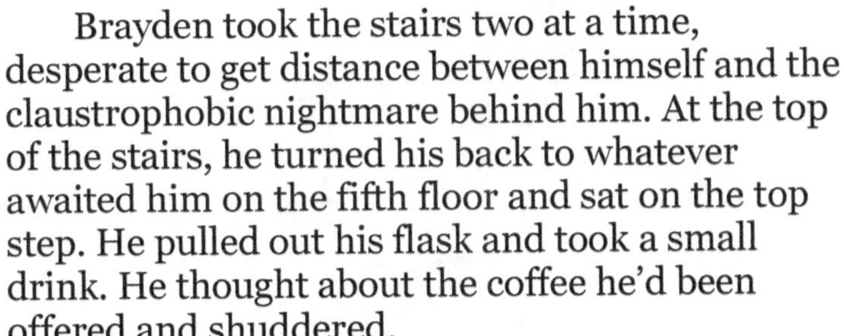

Brayden took the stairs two at a time, desperate to get distance between himself and the claustrophobic nightmare behind him. At the top of the stairs, he turned his back to whatever awaited him on the fifth floor and sat on the top step. He pulled out his flask and took a small drink. He thought about the coffee he'd been offered and shuddered.

Whatever was in the coffee couldn't really have trapped him there with that family. Not really. But it could have drugged him, or poisoned him. Diane admitted to being a killer.

Absently, he ran his fingers over his belt. He had seen some weird shit in this building, *without* any drugs. Really cool shit, some of it, but not stuff you wanted to deal with on drugs. With that thought, the lights abruptly blinked out.

"*Fuck*," Brayden muttered.

"I didn't," said a man's pleading voice in his ear. "You gotta' believe me."

Brayden jerked his head to see who had spoken, and the lights winked back on to show an empty hallway. He was standing, somehow, in front of the wall. He glanced at the stairs, where he had been sitting.

Teleporting. That was new.

He tilted his head back to read the weeping message in front of him.

Untitled
Uchechukwu Onyedikam

midnight prayers
evil eyes lurking in the dark
feeding my fears with blood
dragging me to an unholy savior –
corrupted my salvation

5. The Student

F.K. Marlowe

The door wasn't locked. It swung open at Brayden's touch, onto a room sunk in shadow. A tall, angular figure stood at the barred window, where a little grey light seeped in. Its head was bent over, as though trying to read, by this meagre illumination, the heavy vellum book it held.

At the sound of the door opening, it raised its head and turned.

"Ah, a visitor," it murmured, and its voice was silken, dark as roast coffee. Sinuous, it moved to a little alcove at the back wall of the cell, and laid down the book. Brayden heard the snick of a match being struck, saw a flame flicker and catch. In its glow, he could make out something of the creature's clothing: a scarlet suit, moulded tightly to its lithe form, patterned in delicate criss-crossed lines of darker red.

The creature turned, regarded him by the light of its candle. The flame, held beneath its chin, illuminated a face of ruined beauty. The eyes, glittering darkly in the candle's glow, were difficult to meet.

"Oh," the silken voice murmured, "A human." Its contempt brushed Brayden like thorns.

"Yes, I'm human," he rankled, "Come to hear your story. Tell me how you came to be here!"

"You do not command me to speak, fool!" the creature laughed, its voice warm as blood, "My words command you to listen."

"Alright then," Brayden replied, "Speak, and I will!"

The creature inclined its head, gestured to a low couch along the wall by the door.

"You will want to sit," it invited. "It is a long, gruesome tale, and you humans are so weak." Brayden ignored the jibe and sat, noting the fine silk throw that covered the couch. He waited expectantly, as the creature set the candle in the alcove and turned to stare once more through the window's bars, its back turned so the candlelight played strangely over the odd patterning of its scarlet suit.

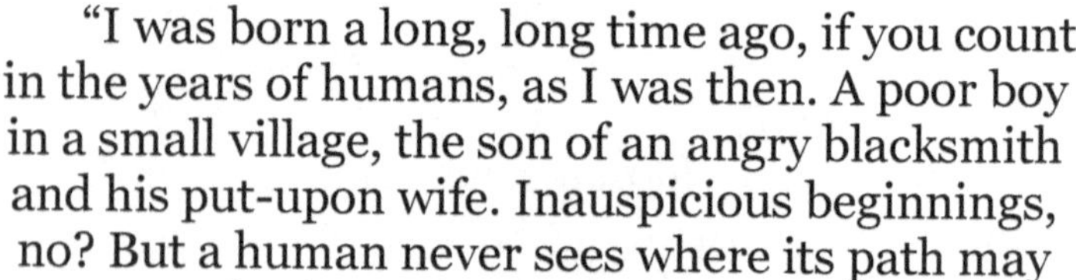

"I was born a long, long time ago, if you count in the years of humans, as I was then. A poor boy in a small village, the son of an angry blacksmith and his put-upon wife. Inauspicious beginnings, no? But a human never sees where its path may lead, only where it has been.

"Life was poor and hard, back then, for most people. My memories are of cold, hunger and dirt, the clanging of iron and the violence of my parents' quarrels. I grew up a small, scared creature, trained by experience to bolt into knotholes at the approach of danger.

"What drove me from home that day, down the dusty path that led out of the village, into the haven of the forest? I don't remember. It wasn't the first time I'd sought refuge in the trees. The other children did not dare to venture into the woods; they whispered of a spirit that dwelt there. But dread was already an old companion to me, with my home a furnace of rage and fear. What creature could be worse than my father's wrath, or my mother's tears?

"I ducked into the shadow of the leaves and felt my soul calm on the instant. The crashing of iron and the hissing of the smithy fire faded and died as my feet hurried me out of sight. All the sounds here were gentle: the call of unseen birds, the lapping of a brook somewhere. Sunlight dappled the path before me, and summer flowers danced. It was a little paradise. I wanted never to leave."

Here the creature paused and took a deep, long breath, as though smelling again the scent of summer woodland. The thick sweetness of longing was in the air, falling on Brayden like the torpor of an August afternoon. He shook his head to clear it of the creature's influence, forcing himself to listen to its words with a critical coldness. This was, after all, one of the damned.

It continued, in a voice like the purr of a tiger. "I don't know how long I wandered, picking early berries and swishing away brambles with sticks I pretended were swords. The shadows were lengthening, the golden light becoming chill. I would have to return home soon, or take my chances out here, in the cold of night. My soul – yes, I still had a soul then – curdled at the thought. I wandered deeper into the woodland's heart than I ever had before, prolonging the evil moment.

"The light was waning when I came upon a little hovel. Raised from the forest itself, a tangle of branches and bines, it was a cruder dwelling even than the low stone huts of the shepherds on the hills above the village. Before it, in a small clearing, a fire burned. Its smoke was pungent, enticing. The smell of food made my empty stomach clench, and the fumes of calming herbs emboldened me."

"'Hello?' I called out, the sound startling in the quiet of the trees. A rook took flight, cawing its annoyance.

"'Good evening, young master,' came a voice from the hovel, and an aged figure stooped into the last of the evening's light. It wore the sackcloth garments of a hermit, the cowl of a druid, and it leaned on a thick staff engraved with strange markings. 'Will you share a bowl of stew with me, and stand me company for my evening meal?'

"It did not need to bid me twice. I say 'it', for I could not yet discern whether the face in the hood's deep shadow belonged to a man or a woman. I later learned that this was a question that occupies only the mortal and foolish, but to me, then, it mattered, for how was I to be polite if I did not know whether to call it Mistress or Sir?

"'Call me Teacher,' it said, as if reading my mind, 'I've been waiting for you.'

"There are two versions of what happened then," the creature continued, and its voice took on the lilt of a lullaby, so that Brayden found himself digging fingernail marks in his palms to keep his mind sharp.

"In the simple one, the one that most humans would see if they watched, we shared a meal and my teacher scratched their staff in the dirt of the forest floor, teaching me my letters. In this version, I stayed only a few days with this strange, old creature, learning quickly; a bright boy with an apt tutor.

"You must decide for yourself whether the other version is more, or less, real.

"In the second version of the tale, I went with them as night overtook the world and we plunged through time to a place beyond it. They showed me wonders your human mind cannot comprehend: the births of stars and planets, the living force that drives the flower to bloom, the fatal breath that withers the fruit on the bough. They taught me the names of angels and demons, names of power that compelled spirits to come at my hest. With them, I heard the music of the spheres, and it changed the very blood in my veins, the tissues of my body, and the fabric of my soul. When I left, I still looked like a human boy, but I was a creature of a different kind.

"I did not know why they had chosen me. All I cared was that I was no longer weak. I no longer needed to fear the anger of petty humans like my father, with his crude fists, his belt, his paltry smithy furnace.

"My steps, on the path back to the village, were sure and firm. I swung open the door to our cottage and stood defiant in the doorway, ready to show my father his power over me was gone.

"Ah, fool I was still," the creature murmured, and its head dropped. "For he had one power over me yet, one human weakness lodged within me, and he had taken full advantage of it. In his rage at my absence, he had turned upon my mother. She lay on the swept dirt floor in her own drying blood, her face so broken and bruised I could not look on it.

"I did not need to touch her skin to know it long cold. My teacher had shown me how to discern the pulse of life that quickens in the air about all living things. I did not feel it here. Instead, the rank chill of death seeped from my mother's body. Mine was overcome with a rage I have scarcely felt since, in all my long, long years of existence.

"I strode from the cottage, my child's body shaking with wrath. Straight into the smithy, unflinching, as my father turned from the furnace where the stink of molten metal rose up acrid in the morning air.

"'You're back, are you, dung rat?' he sneered, 'Belly get the better of you, did it?'

"'What have you done to my mother?' I asked, and if he were less coarse and stupid, the ice in my voice must have given him pause, for it was not the voice of a ten-year-old boy.

"'Taught her a lesson, like the one I'll teach you. She lacked respect.'

"'She's dead.'

"He shrugged, 'One less useless mouth to feed.'

"The last of the child in me took over then, and I flew at him with my little fists flailing. I beat and kicked for all I was worth, but he was a mountain of a man and he just laughed at me. Then, calmly and slowly, as if he were dipping a horseshoe in water to cool it, he took my head and held my face against the hot stone of the furnace.

"I smelt my own flesh burn. There was a moment of searing pain, and then my mind filled with the vastness of the stars, and my teacher's voice was in my ears, reminding me of all I had learned.

"I muttered one of the many secret words they'd taught me, and a strength flowed through me greater than the pain or the heat of the fire. I lifted my father's hand from my head as though it were no heavier than a leaf. For one moment that lives in my memory still, as fresh as when I saw it, I gazed on his face. Oh, I cannot describe to you the sweetness of his look – horror and disbelief and thwarted anger all combined. I tell you; I have looked upon angels, and I never saw a face that gladdened my heart more.

"I plunged my fingers into the smithy fire and lifted out a handful of flame. My father backed away, fear bright on his face, and I took the gentlest of breaths, then pursed my lips and blew, softly, as though only whistling.

"The flame wound from my hand like a skein of silk. He saw it coming and tried to run, but it twined itself around him like a clinging vine. He fell to the floor and I stood over him while he screamed and burned. It took a long time. I made sure of that. I poured into the flames all the years of pain and fear he'd visited upon my mother and me. How he writhed and howled! I tell you, mortal, it was sweeter to me than the music of the spheres. I wanted it to go on forever."

The creature's mouth became a rictus grin and, as it luxuriated in its memories, Brayden smelt burning flesh, felt the creature's exhilaration make his own head swim. He fought it down, fingers twisting in the couch's silken throw.

"I could've stayed, I suppose," the creature went on. "Told people of the terrible accident my father had suffered, in his smithy. A moment's inattention in the grip of a hangover. Gone on with my little village life. I didn't consider it for a second.

"Instead, I lifted my hands and the flames of the smithy furnace rose like the notes of an orchestra. I walked out of the conflagration, down the village street, the fire following me like a river in spate. The screams of the people as they burned were music.

"You will find no trace of that village on any map. You could sift the soil with the finest of sieves and detect no remnant of any living thing. I erased my origins entirely. I was no longer a weak human, born in dirt. I had rebirthed myself in fire and blood." The creature smiled in satisfaction, savouring its memories. Brayden stared at it, afraid to wonder what path it had taken next.

"For a while, I wandered the countryside. I avoided humanity, with its petty frailties and tawdry aspirations. I sought my teacher, sometimes, when the smoke of a campfire crossed my path, but I never found them, not then. I discovered my own way to dig through time to the place beneath, and continued learning. My powers grew. For a while, I was sated and calm. There is a peace that comes with great knowledge, enough to quiet even my wrath." The creature's silken voice softened to a hiss. Brayden shivered.

"Then one evening, I strayed close to a village not unlike the one where I was born. I even strained my ears for the clanging of a smithy, but instead, music floated to me on the air. Not the music of the spheres, but a human voice, sweet, and warm with life.

"A shard of human weakness stirred in me, gouged at my heart. I followed the voice as though it were an incantation that had me in thrall.

"What shall I tell you? I found a woman, her hair as bright as smithy flames, gathering herbs at dusk. Her campfire burned with their aromatic smoke. She was a healer, a witch, her powers a dim reflection of my own. But where I was cold and inhuman, she was sultry with life. I fell in love with her, and she with me. We were happy for a little time. I told her my story, and she said that I had learned anger and hatred well; now was the time to learn love. I thought, perhaps, there was a value to be had in mere mortality, after all.

"Alas, to be mortal is to fear. That is perhaps the hardest lesson of all to truly learn, though every living creature knows it, instinctively, from its birth. Why did I allow myself this weakness? Fool."

The creature turned away in disgust, as if to hide its shame.

Brayden burned with curiosity. "What did you fear?"

"What every mortal fears. Loss." The creature turned its face to Brayden once more, its expression almost human. "Losing her to another, of course."

"So, I reached back to my earliest lessons, when my teacher scratched their staff in the ground to show me the power of words. A power you barely even guess at. I wrote a love spell, a simple thing, to keep her mine alone. Not worthy of my talents, you might say. And yet it seemed to work, for a while. She was content to stay near me always, never wandering beyond my sight as she collected her plants or brewed her potions. 'See,' she would tell me, as she coaxed a seed to green life, 'Creation and destruction are points on a great wheel,' and I smiled that she, with her poor herbs and her grandam's charms for the birthing of babes, should presume to lecture me."

The creature flicked a finger and a spark leapt from the candle, kindling into a vision. Brayden knew he was peering into the past as clearly as if he looked through a window. A flame-haired woman and a young man that he realised, with surprise, was the creature as he must have been, laughed and kissed, before the vision sputtered like candlelight, reforming.

Now the woman stood before the man, a crumpled paper in her hands, and ice in her voice. "How could you?" she demanded, shaking the paper at him like an accusation. "Our power is not for this! Love is not this!"

"But I did it for love!" pleaded the man.

"How do you know," she demanded, "That I ever truly loved you? That it wasn't just the effect of your spell?" She turned to leave, and the man grasped her wrists. Brayden saw her lips move, and the paper in her hands turn to flames. The man sprang back, staring in shock at her unscathed hands, at his own as they blistered and blackened.

"I wondered for the first time who she really was," murmured the creature as the woman walked away, the vision fading around her. "I sought her for years. I did not find her."

It fell silent, remembering. Candlelight flickered across the strange markings on its back.

"Despair grows slowly, like a rot. You must know this, mortal. It affects even your kind. For me, awake to the light and dark at the centre of all things, shadows eclipsed all but the fire of destruction. My mind revolved around the memory of my village in flames. This, at least, was a pleasure still open to me, a worthy use of my powers.

"I began rather theatrically. I scratched words into the earth and watched other villages burn, towns, cities. My runes raised wars, and I wandered through their bloody aftermath exalting. The disembowelled dead, the agonised dying: these were balm for my soul.

"Eventually, though, I tired of such crude use of my talents. I wanted more. For humans to be the source of their own misery; to know, like me, the torment of regret.

"This is the true power of words, mortal. The whisper that twines itself around the brain, spawning doubts, ambitions, suspicions. Plots and vengeances. The scribbled note that changes the course of a life; of a hundred, a thousand lives.

"I made my home among humans again, threw myself into their petty jockeyings for power. I could, of course, have made myself an emperor and enslaved them, but it was far more gratifying to watch them forge their own shackles. I lived as a lesser courtier, a man of means but not of ambition. Positioned myself at a tangent to the centre of power, the better to exploit those yearning for it. I whispered secrets. Planted hopes, doubts and fears. Oh, how they squirmed in the nets of their own making!" The creature laughed, a sound like breaking glass. The room in the air had turned so chill that Brayden could see his own breath. It was a comfort, reminding him that he was still alive.

"Then, an opportunity arose that was worthy of my skills. I found a woman as ambitious as she was ruthless. A lady of the court, accomplished, vain, determined. There were many like her, willing to connive, to deceive, to betray, for influence. But from first meeting, I sensed that nothing would baulk this one in her desire for power.

"One word, only, breathed in her drowsing ear, was enough to set her on her course. You may say this is no proof of my power, that she barely needed me to bring her to ruin, but oh! With my help, she did so much more than that. She brought a country to burn.

"How, you ask? How was this woman, in a world still ruled by men, to exert her desires? Why, through a male instrument, of course. And yet the King was married, and loved his wife. What to do?

"I whispered the thought that her conceited King loved his wife for the copper glint of her hair, so like his own. The words were mine, the power mine, but the alchemy that kindled Lady Anne's swart locks to fiery auburn was all her own. The flame she kindled in the King's loins was more commonplace, for she already had a score of would-be lovers. So much the better. An egotistical man likes nothing better than to win a woman from other men, like a dog with a bone. And so he pursued her like a hound at hunt.

"Now I murmured to her uncle, her brother. 'Look to the Lady's honour. The King would make her his whore.' Little I cared. Less cared they. But the seed of my suggestion was planted. The King had many dalliances, many ladies bewhored to his desires. How was this lady to take a more prominent position on the chess board?

"'The King always gets his wish,' I whispered in their minds, as they slept. 'Think what influence on a man like that, to be once denied, to be long denied, and yet to remain desiring!' So they set Lady Anne on a tightrope that would have defeated many. She walked it as if it were the pretty paths that wound through the rose gardens at court.

"And in the King's ear, my phantom words, lodged in other men's mouths, poured doubt.

"'You must have an heir!'

"'You grow no younger, Lord King! Nor does your Lady Wife!'

"'If some accident were to befall the Queen...'

"'If, God forbid, some accident befell you...'

"Perhaps you know the story, albeit told a different way: how a lustful, besotted King tore down the Church, shattered the calm of his people, and set his country, perhaps the world, on an entirely different course?

"Not a King. Me.

"In short, the King cast off his loving wife and took the scheming Lady for his new Queen. His country roiled in shock, but the Lady had her desire: she was Lady no longer. She was Queen.

"Only one thing now was needed to seal her victory. She must give the King what his former wife could not: a male heir. But another whisper went about the court, one that did not even come from my lips. Ah, sweet fortune! Such a word as this would have been deadly to the speaker, if overheard, for its power was as great as any charm I could have raised.

"The King is impotent."

Here the creature paused and turned to Brayden, its eyes closed, rapt in memory. The candle cast a fiery glow upon its face, illuminating the haunting mixture of beauty and ruin there. The curved lips parted in a long sigh, and it opened eyes that gleamed like black pools in the flickering light.

"You see the elegance of it? The joy? To give the tiniest push here, the softest nudge there; a muttered sentence, a murmured word. This was my master work. I was the unseen spider in a web invisible to those who struggled in its strands, thinking themselves free. It was," the creature paused, sighed once more, "Exquisite.

"Queen Anne found a way, as she always had. She quickened with child. Some muttered the calumny that it was the seed of a lover, not the

King. Others breathed a different, damning truth. The babe was born of witchcraft."

The glittering obsidian of the creature's eyes flickered to meet Brayden's.

"Yes. My doing. I ensured the Queen discovered me, at last. Enough to intrigue her, then to hope, and finally to place her trust, her very life, in my hands.

"'Use your art to give me a babe that will rule longer and brighter than any can imagine!' She promised me jewels, influence. Hah! As if there were any power in her gift not already mine for the taking. But I agreed the terms she offered.

"I kept the deal, after a fashion. A babe she wanted, a babe was born. I see from your face, you know my little joke. Of course, the child was a girl. It would rule, as Anne requested, but neither she nor the King would live to see that come to pass.

"How she raged! Oh, it was marvellous to see! The King had gambled all for an heir and now he had another useless girl! What good was a daughter, he stormed! Girls did not have the brains to rule! Poor, fat fool. Who did he think ruled now? It wasn't he.

"Indeed, the Queen bent all her new powers upon me in her vengeance. She pursued me like a fox, and like a fox I hid, laughing as the hunt passed me by. Like a fox, I watched and waited, until the time was right to sneak into the chicken coop and spill a little blood.

"The King must have a male heir. This time Anne was very clear in her demands. She sought out another with the forbidden power she'd bought of me. A woman with hair redder than her own, red as the flames of a fire in woodland. A woman I knew well. One of the few with the power to ruin my plans.

"She came to me, when she'd done it, my lover from so long ago.

"'I have righted the wrong you did,' she said, and her eyes sparked with the anger I remembered from the morning she set my spell ablaze and scorched the hands that wrought it.

"'The King shall have his heir; the country shall be spared more of your evil.' The creature's voice turned bittersweet as he mouthed the words of his former love.

"'What have you become?' she asked me then. 'All the power you were given, the knowledge of all hidden things. The secrets of the universe, and you have used them thus.' She begged me, turn back. Become what I once was.

"'What?' I asked her. 'A wretch ensnared by love, bound in fear?'

"She shook her head and left, the smell of a woodsmoke fire trailing after, like a memory I could not yet quite place.

"And I watched her leave, again. How dared she? How dared she pit her power against mine? I did not know then, how I underestimated her, as the King underestimated his Queen. His vengeance, when he knew, would work Anne's destruction, from the same root that now wrought mine.

"The child quickened in Anne's belly. The court and country rejoiced. This time the heir would be a boy, and peace could come at last. All my plans laid to ruin.

"No!"

The creature stood, remembering. Candlelight flickered over its face, a play of emotions. Brayden saw arrogance, pride, and something else. Fear. Doubt. The little hairs on the back of his neck prickled and he glanced at the door, checking it was still open. He felt the full danger of the creature now, as if it were a wild animal that might spring on him at any moment. He shifted his weight, edged minutely toward the exit. The creature, bound up in its memories, did not notice.

"For this last magic," it continued, "I needed all my power. I went to my book, the one you saw me reading. In it, I had inscribed all my learning over the long centuries of my life, but now I did more. I poured into it my very soul."

"The words on its pages kindled and burned into life. They grew wings. They were new creatures, beautiful and terrible. I stroked them, breathed sweet upon them. My loves."

The creature gestured to the heavy book that rested in the alcove under the candle's shifting light. At the movement of its hand, black shapes, spindly and winged like insects, lifted themselves from the fluttering pages and swarmed into the air, circling the creature like a maelstrom until the strange scarlet figure was almost lost to view, and other images flickered and formed in the darkness at the centre of the cloud of beating wings.

Brayden saw a timbered room and in it, a figure both familiar and strange. The creature was a man again, in the thick velvet coat and breeches of an old-time merchant. In the vision, the insect-like creatures flittered and buzzed indistinctly and the man-who-was-the-creature stared at them, rapt.

"Fly," he breathed. "Go to the Queen, to the child in her belly. Pour into it all my hatred of this world and the stupid, vain mortals who live in it. Twist it and deform it, but make it look fairer than the sun. Make it an aberration. The Queen shall give birth to a demon that will rule this country as if it sits the very throne of hell!"

The hum of the insects grew to an angry rasping like a buzzsaw and the creatures lifted up and swarmed, out of windows and doors, into the street. They streamed through different paths to the palace; dim as shadows, they beat against the leaded windows of the Queen's room as she slept on a great, curtained bed, her hand on her belly. In helpless horror, Brayden watched them wriggle through cracks in the window panes, beneath the sill of the door, weave from the hearth with chimney soot heavy on their wings, so that when they crawled on the snowy white sheets of the Queen's bed they left black smudges like footprints in snow. They massed on the sleeping Queen, a nest of writhing, squirming darkness. Brayden's neck itched, his fingers rubbed at the skin, feeling the crawl of invisible feet, the brush of phantom wings.

"Can you imagine how marvellous that would have been, mortal? All the lands of all the world would have run with blood and fire." The creature paused for a moment, lost in its vision of destruction, and Brayden too beheld a dark figure lift itself up from the belly of the Queen, quiver and elongate. It towered over her and she became not a Queen, not one woman, but a curved landscape of hills and valleys thick with people, over whom the figure's shadow fell like night. Fire radiated from it as though it were the dark centre of some great star, coalescing to molten flame that coursed down inclines, burning all in its path. Screams and groans lifted from the vision, echoing back from the stone walls of the creature's cell, swelling with the howling of winds and the beating of dark wings. The noise grew until it became a living thing, until Brayden clamped his hands over his ears and closed his eyes against the horror of its malevolence and power.

The creature lifted its voice above the roar, so that the screech of it penetrated Brayden's covered ears and drove itself into his brain. "It would have been the apocalypse itself, wrought by my hand!" The vision swirled, the swarming word-insects beating their wings in a frenzy, the shrieking of winds and voices rising until Brayden himself screamed to drown out the sound.

Instantly the room was silent. The vision, the swarm of insects, were gone. In the alcove, the candle flame flickered, and a few pages of the great vellum book fluttered softly, as if in a light breeze.

Brayden heard his own breath in the silence. The creature glanced at him, as though it had forgotten he was there. For a moment, it turned to stare out into the grey dusk that filtered through the bars of its cell, then shifted its gaze back to Brayden, to finish its tale.

"I couldn't think how she discovered my work, my old lover. Now I know who she was, the real extent of her power, it is no mystery, of course. The breath of every life whispered in her ear, and this, the new one her own hand had brought into being, no less. She would have heard the darkness on its voice, the poison I'd wrought in her perfect creation." The creature's mouth twisted in grim satisfaction. Then it passed a hand across its face, and its expression was stricken with defeat.

"The rumours found me before she did. The city was alive with them." Voices arose around Brayden, whispers clamouring for attention, urgent, excited, revelling in the horror of their words.

"The Queen has miscarried!"

"She walked down the corridor to the throne room all unknowing, trailing blood like a stream!"

"The babe was born alive, though it was but three months formed!"

"They say it wailed like a banshee on the stroke of midnight, then died."

"Misshapen it was! Twisted like a serpent!"

"Black as coal!"

"Green as emeralds!"

"Feet like a goat's hooves!"

"Spine cleft open into wings like a bat!"

"Not a babe! A demon!"

"A demon!"

"The Queen has borne a devil!"

The whispers rose to a single hiss, then dissipated like smog, leaving a trace of sulphur in the air.

The creature flicked a finger, and turned away, as smoke wound from the candle flame, twisting itself into a final vision. Brayden felt emotions crackle like sparks from its defiant back and knew it didn't watch not because it lacked interest, but because the scene was wrought so vividly within it that it did not need to.

In the vision, the creature, a man again, sat at a heavy wooden desk, his great book open before him, his head in his hands. In twos and threes, insectile words flickered to rest upon his wrists, his fingers, his head. They nuzzled, consoling, even as they whispered the news of his failure, then forlornly fluttered to take their places in the worn vellum pages.

A heavy door slammed open, a shaft of bright light, like an accusing finger, fell upon the creature-man's bowed head. He didn't even look up as he murmured, "You've found me out, then."

"Yes. You and your plan." The woman's words were calm, but her body vibrated with anger, seeming to blaze like the red of her hair.

"What of it?" the creature-man asked, and finally lifted his head to gaze at her; his love, his heart, his teacher. "It's over. You've won."

The woman shook her head, and the creature-man recoiled under her look of disappointed contempt.

"You understand nothing," she whispered, "Even now."

The creature-man fell to his knees, grasped her hand, begging, "Teach me then! Teach me again! Make me understand!" His voice was not the assured, rich velvet of the creature in the cell with Brayden, but human, broken with weakness and need.

But the woman snatched her hand away and stepped back from him as if he was an unclean thing. "There is no teaching you," she spat. "That error was all mine."

Then she retreated through the door, waving a pale hand, as if in farewell. On the desk, the great book kindled into flames, and the insect-like words rose from it, their wings burning, fluttering about the room in anguish, setting light to all they touched. As Brayden watched, the room and the figure still kneeling in it became a conflagration, one bright mass of fire. It blazed like a starburst, and died into nothingness.

In the centre of the cell, the creature stood silently, its tale done. The candle in its alcove had burned to a stump, its light beginning to gutter. Brayden spoke, his voice rusty from long silence.

"And now you're here. What's your punishment? To read over your life again and again with no power to change the words?"

The creature snickered. "Don't be foolish. That is the fate of every mortal."

"What is your penance then, in this place? What is the fate assigned to you? Finish your story!" Brayden stood, took a few paces toward the creature, then cowered back as it leapt toward him like an angry beast, snarling,

"Fool! I am not being punished. This is my paradise! Here, I am the one with the power. My words fly out into the world and do my bidding. I feed them, I send them from this window, and none can stop me! Not even her!"

From the charred pages of the great vellum book, came a screeching, a flapping of wings as the words lifted themselves and fluttered toward Brayden. He watched in fascination, unable to move as one black shape flickered onto his palm, slicing its wings into his flesh. A trickle of blood ran across his skin, and a dark line appeared.

He backed toward the door, almost falling out of it as he struggled to slam it shut on the insects swarming toward him. From inside its cell the creature, clothed only in blood and scars, shrieked in laughter at his fear.

Brayden's body was heavy with fatigue as he made his way up toward the sixth floor, trying to shake off the creature's story as he went. All that magic and cursing. And those *bugs*. He fought the urge to strip right there on the stairs, to make sure there weren't any little hitchhikers under his clothes.

As he climbed, he became aware of a scraping noise – not an even, machine-made sound, but an uneven scratching, like someone using a tool to scratch stone.

The tang of copper, never very far from his senses in this place, grew stronger as he got to the top of the stairs, along with the scraping, which sounded like it was right above–

Brayden looked up to see a figure like the so-called shadow people the paranormal nerds talked about. The thing had been crawling along the ceiling, back and forth, in front of the writing scrawled on the hallway wall. Its claws scraped along the plaster, sending little motes of plaster dust floating to the carpet.

As if aware it had company, it stopped and turned its head toward Brayden where he stood reading the words it seemed to be guarding. It must have been startled to see him, because it was suddenly grabbing frantically at the ceiling for purchase, before it lost that battle and fell.

Brayden jumped back and watched it flail past him and disappear silently into the floor. He hurried for the door up ahead.

Untitled
IrrationalPoet

came around
to call again

master of war
king of hate
rules us all
and chose our fate

we the bearers of
horror bring we
be the end of all
living things

and in the blood
that coats this land
shivers now
my dying hand

VII
JUSTICE

6. The Priest

Marc Tizura

Brayden marched down the long, cavernous hallway in a slight daze as it seemed to shift, as if turning upside down and slowly correcting itself.

He scarcely noticed the floor had given way to cobblestones as he entered the vestibule and stopped at a pair of large wooden doors that reminded him of a medieval castle – planks of wood, iron hinges, iron studs, and two iron rings for door handles. He grabbed a ring and pulled. The door didn't budge.

He tried pushing, and the door gave way with a groan of ancient wood and metal. He steeled himself, the best he could, for whatever lay beyond. He had seen so much unexplainable shit since he entered The Hyperion. "Ever forward," he said to himself as he entered.

Brayden walked into a small stone chapel. Rows of pews, with an aisle down the center, faced a raised stage. On the stage sat an altar draped in a white linen cloth, a gold cross at its center. Behind the altar were three stained glass windows of red and white glass, the center one slightly taller than the others. Flanking the altar on the left was the Virgin Mary holding the baby Jesus. On the right, Saint Joseph. All three faces had been melted to unrecognizable blurs. In front of the stage was a large man dressed all in black.

A priest, Brayden thought.

The priest's hair was a tousled mop of dark curls. He prayed in a deep booming voice.

*"PATER noster, qui es in cœlis; sanctificetur nomen tuum. Adveniat regnum tuum. Fiat voluntas tua...*come in all the way, Mr. Winchell. One shouldn't linger in doorways. It's rude, and bad form," the Priest said.

Brayden entered further as the priest resumed his prayer.

"...sicut in cœlo, et in terra. Panem nostrum quotidianum da nobis hodie," droned the Priest.

Brayden stopped at a marble bowl on a stand that held holy water. The old axiom of his youth took over as he dipped his two fingers in it to the bottom.

"Et dimitte nobis debita nostra, sicut et nos dimittimus debitoribus nostris," the Priest recited.

Brayden removed his fingers from the font to find that they were dry. The Priest let out a rueful chuckle. Brayden shrugged and walked down the aisle to sit in the second row from the front. He saw a rosary in the Priest's hands. The Priest had fallen silent. He turned his head only slightly, acknowledging Brayden's presence, but still faced the twisted trio before him. Brayden licked his dry lips as his fingers ran over the notches of his belt.

"Aren't you going to ask?" the Priest asked.

"A priest in Hell," Brayden began with a smirk, "What did you do? Touch kids?"

The Priest emitted another humorless chuckle. Something in the sound chilled Brayden, causing his heart to race and his stomach to drop. He clenched his jaw and tightened his fists, letting anger and contempt take the place of the fear.

"Not exactly," the Priest said.

"All right, so what's your story, holy man," Brayden asked.

"It was 1987 when I came to The Hyperion. Before that, I was an up-and-coming priest assigned to the Vatican, when a special assignment crossed my desk," the Priest began.

A wave of vertigo washed over Brayden as the room swirled and changed to show the Priest's story.

The Priest sat at a large oak desk, stacks of books open all around him as he shuffled through papers. A cigarette hung loosely between his lips as he read, mouthing along with one of the many papers he held.

A series of loud knocks on the door broke his concentration. Startled, he dropped the cigarette into his lap. He hissed and uttered a small cuss as he wiped the ashes from his pants.

A stately man in white robes and a small red skull cap strolled in. He extended a hand to the Priest. The Priest took the hand and kissed the ornate ring that he wore.

"*Buongiorno,* Excellency," the Priest said.

"*Buongiorno,* Padre Belton," the Cardinal replied.

"I was not expecting Your Excellency. Please sit down," Belton said, gesturing to the chair across from the desk.

"I cannot, I'm afraid. I must be brief," the Cardinal replied apologetically.

He produced a stack of file folders and handed them to Belton, who took them and began to thumb through them.

"There has been a series of incidents in America involving these priests and... and children," The Cardinal began.

Belton's face paled, his eyes widening and his mouth dropping open in sudden comprehension as he continued to look at the file folder.

"You are to go to these plants to remove these individuals, find them new plants, and insist on sabbaticals before they start those new assignments," The Cardinal continued.

Horror filled Belton's eyes as he put the folders down on his desk. The Cardinal gave a sympathetic nod of understanding.

"It is not an easy assignment, but I expect you to do it quickly and quietly, before the media gets a hold of it. For the good of all the Church," The Cardinal said.

"For the good of all the Church, Your Excellency," Belton echoed stiffly.

The Cardinal blessed him by making the sign of the cross before him, and Belton crossed himself. The Cardinal extended his hand and Belton once again took it and kissed the ornate ring.

"Go with God, Thomas," The Cardinal said as he departed.

Father Thomas Belton, with trembling hands, lit another cigarette as the image shifted and swirled.

Belton sat in a black sedan outside of a church. Rain pounded on the roof and pelted off the windshield as the wipers cracked noisily. A folder lay open against the steering wheel. His eyes kept darting to the church door as he read and reread the file, over and over again.

Red-hot fire filled him as he read. It started in his stomach, moved its way up to settle in his chest, caused his eyes to burn, his jaw to clench, and his teeth to grind. He had a white-knuckle death grip on the steering wheel as the trunk opened and closed. The front passenger door opened and an elderly priest in a fedora and overcoat slid in. He was dripping wet. A coldness came over Belton, an inkling of an idea, not yet fully formed, scratched inside his head as he looked over at the other priest.

"Father Burger?" Belton asked.

"Yes. You are Father Belton?" Burger asked.

"Correct," Belton said flatly.

"God bless you! God bless the Holy Father in Rome for this second chance! To take me away from temptation! I beg the Lord's forgiveness!" Burger said, on the verge of tears.

Belton felt his stomach roil and turn as he started to drive. He drove on autopilot, as if guided by an unknown force. He pulled into an alley and put the car in park.

"What!? What are we doing?" Burger asked, frightened.

"Get out," Belton said, coldly.

"What!?" Burger cried.

"GET OUT!" Belton roared.

"I...I...I don't understand!" Burger cried.

Belton got out of the car, slammed the door, and stormed to the other side. He flung Burger's door open. Burger let out a small cry of alarm as Belton reached in, seizing him and yanking him out.

He threw Burger to the ground hard. Burger let out an *oof* and a cry. Burger tried to get up, but Belton brought his foot down hard on the side of his knee. There was a crunching noise and a snap. Burger howled and tried to crawl away.

Belton seized the older man by the collar of his coat and slammed him into the car. Burger yelped as he made impact with a metallic thud. He panted, raising his hands in supplication.

"I have sinned!" Belton yelled over the rain, pointing an accusing finger. Hot spittle flew from his mouth, hitting Burger in the face.

Burger whined and began to sob. Belton smacked him across the face.

"Say it!" Belton demanded.

"I have sinned!" Burger cried.

Burger began to blubber like a child. Belton turned his back, his teeth bared as he tried to control the fury that threatened to overwhelm him. Then he saw the wire. He went to it as Burger pleaded into the rain. His voice seemed distant, almost inaudible. Belton picked the wire up and steel resolve filled him. He went back to the blubbering, begging, and pleading man in the rain with the wire in his hand.

"In my thoughts and in my words," Belton whispered coldly next to Burger's ear.

"In my thoughts and in my words," Burger cried.

"What I have done and what I have failed to do," Belton snarled.

"What I have done and what I have fail—" Burger began, learning forward.

Belton had moved into position and snaked the wire around Burger's neck, now tightening it. Burger thrashed. Kicked out. Clawed at the wire. Clawed at Belton's hand. Belton held firm. Burger gurgled and gasped. His eyes bulged wide in their sockets. Burger gave one final gurgle as Belton twisted the wire. There was a crunch. A snap. Burger went limp. Belton removed the wire from the other man's neck. He stared down at the cold, lifeless body, its wide, unblinking eyes frozen with fear. And it came to him. His holy mission.

There were twelve priests in the folders, twelve disciples, twelve tribes of Israel, twelve levels of heaven, twelve orders of angels. He was filled with exaltation, a sense of divine purpose. He was made anew, a knight of the holiest order, to deliver God's wrath upon these sinners. And this, he looked at the wire, was his holy weapon.

He got back into the car and drove off as the image swirled again.

Another crying priest knelt before an altar. Blood ran from his lip and nose. Belton lorded over him with wire in hand. Belton's knuckles were smeared with that priest's blood.

"I didn't hurt any of them... I loved... them," the bloodied priest cried.

"You can tell that to the Almighty when you stand before the throne," Belton said, calmly.

The bloodied priest began to cry harder.

"Now, where were we? Ah yes, I am heartily sorry I have offended thee and detest all my sins, say it," Belton growled.

"No! No, I won't!" The bloodied priest sobbed.

"Suit yourself," Belton said, wrapping the wire around the bloody priest's neck, "Because I dread the loss of Heaven and pain of Hell."

The image shifted and swirled again. There were other victims in the swirl. Brayden counted at least six before it stopped.

Belton was hunched over, cupping his balls. A mixture of pain and rage danced on his face. He bared his teeth and groaned, which turned into a growl. His bloodshot eyes were surrounded by dark circles. He looked like a man who didn't sleep much these days. The young priest, who had dealt Belton the blow, fled with his long hair flapping in the wind.

With a grunt of effort, Belton pushed himself off the wall he had been leaning against and gave chase. Belton was right on the young priest's heels. He reached out, grabbing the long hair and pulling him back. Belton threw him to the ground and began to kick and stomp the young priest's face. When Belton was satisfied, he stopped and straddled the young priest.

Grabbing a fistful of the young priest's shirt, Belton lifted him up to look him directly in his face.

"So that face loosened a lot of young girls' skirts, did it?" Belton snarled.

The young priest hocked back in his throat and spat a bloody wad of phlegm in Belton's face. Belton grimaced, nodded, and wrapped the wire around his neck.

The images shifted and swirled. Victim after victim after victim. Brayden's stomach lurched to watch. He counted at least twenty in all. The image stopped at Belton's office in the Vatican.

Belton was almost unrecognizable from the man he had been when he left. His hair was wild and unkempt. His eyes were wary and unfocused; they kept darting around the room. The dark circles under his eyes were much worse than before. He looked emaciated.

He bared his teeth and snarled at the door. The door had been barricaded. It rattled in its hinges as people on the other side slammed into it, trying to gain entry.

On his desk was a lantern and above his desk there was a noose.

"Padre Belton, this is Polizia! Open the door, Padre," a voice said from the other side of the door.

"I am a knight of God!" Belton roared.

"Make it easy on yourself, Padre," the voice said.

Yes, he would. He would make it easy on himself. Surely God would welcome his true, faithful, and noble servant home with open arms. He went to the desk and climbed to the noose.

He kicked over the lantern, and the books and papers caught fire almost immediately. He put the noose around his neck and stepped off. The last sound he heard was his neck breaking.

He quickly realized something was wrong. Something was very, very wrong. There was supposed to be a light at the end of the tunnel, not this pitch black...what was that screaming...oh God...no...

Brayden stared in wide-eyed alarm at Belton, who remained kneeling before the altar. "I think you should get a medal," Brayden said, hoarsely.

"You think so?" Belton said with contempt, "I thought I would get my crown in heaven, but as I found out, murder is murder, no matter how you justify it. It seems God doesn't work like the

American legal system. You do something, you pay for it. No matter how you dress it up."

"I'm not sure–" Brayden began.

"Not sure! Doubting Thomas! All the wonders and horrors you have seen?! It's that...that..." Belton sniffed the air like a hunting dog scenting prey, "foolish pride, and pride cometh before the fall."

Brayden's body broke out in gooseflesh as Belton continued to scent the air. Belton began to snarl and growl. Brayden's heart raced in his chest, beating like a jackhammer. He wanted to get up, but he seemed frozen to the pew.

"I smell your other sins, Mr. Winchell. The foul stench of depravity oozes from you," Belton growled.

"Smell? Don't you mean see? Smell my sins, like some bloodhound," Brayden attempted to joke.

Brayden's forced laughter died in his throat as Belton rose to his feet, turned, and faced him. Brayden's mouth hung open in a silent scream.

Belton had no eyes. Where his eyes had been, there was healed scar tissue and skin.

"Smelled, Mr. Winchell! They made me eat my eyes in Hell! They will do worse to you when you join us!" Belton roared.

The altar and statues burst into flames. The stained glass exploded and shards of glass flew everywhere. The flames leapt up, catching Belton on fire, engulfing him. Belton howled.

Brayden's paralysis broke and he fled the chapel to the sound of Belton's screams, which echoed and chased him down the hallway to the stairs that would take him to the next floor.

His lungs burned. The muscles in his legs burned. He felt like he had just climbed twenty floors, rather than twenty steps. Twice, he stumbled as he climbed, catching himself on his hands and crawling his way back upright.

All the weird stuff he couldn't explain was getting to him, too. Some of it, he was almost ready to believe at this point.

"No, no, no," he chided himself. "That's bullshit. There's an explanation for everything."

"*Are you sure?*" A voice that sounded like his own whispered back at him, blood-stained breath tickling his ear.

Brayden's hands balled into fists at his sides. "Stop hiding! Come out and face me like a goddamn man!"

His bravado was met with silence. Gradually, he unballed his fists. "That's what I thought," he grumbled.

He approached the message on the wall and read.

Blood Moon

C.E. Wallace

Under blood red skies
dragging specters
    one   by   one
out of the depths
of mind crypts
    the vaults
haunted with
    grief and guilt

screams of
past and future
echo in the dark well
    of   my   mind
tormented souls
dragging chains
    of regret and fear
bonds of guilt
    laced with poison

shadow work
eclipses hope
     as the moon
slips beneath earth's
     cloak   of   darkness
light and dark
at war for a brief
     moment in time

this too
     shall pass

7. I'm Not Making Any Excuses

Laura A. Cooney

By the time Brayden reached the door, his pounding heart had slowed from his terrified flight. The hallway on this floor was pregnant with an eerie silence like the aftermath of a scream. The door had a thick window of institutional glass embedded with wire security mesh. It looked heavy and very high-security, but the handle turned easily in his hand.

The door opened into a narrow room, apparently uninhabited. Squares of brighter paint on the walls showed where pictures, or artwork, had hung. A larger square of different brickwork looked like a picture window had been closed in at some point. A bookshelf in the corner stood dusty and empty. And in the center of the room, a single folding chair, with a sheaf of much-thumbed pages. Brayden shrugged and picked the papers up. He sat and flipped through quickly before settling in to read.

I was present at the birth of my children.

What it took to grow them was never returned to me. The balls of pure starlight that exited became atomic and grew. The power I once held within me transferred to these entities and overtook them. I'm desolate to say, I didn't handle it well.

I'm not making any excuses.

It was a Wednesday, and the street was thick with rain. My body was both watching Barbie and listening to Frozen songs with child one. Meanwhile, the other one was screaming, 'I want beans,' from the play kitchen. The last thing I remember is wishing someone would come and cut the electricity off.

And that's when I snapped. Whatever thread was holding my fragile sanity onto the mothership came loose and the anchor crashed off the hull. When I came to, I saw the monster I had become. They lay still for the first time since 4am, together, blood on their tiny faces.

In my mind, they were hugging as they used to, but the judge told me they were clinging. For life, much good it did them.

And that's what brought me here. Writing this unsettling tale in this unsettling format. I murdered my own children in a rage on a wet Wednesday afternoon because I was exhausted and empty. A husk, what is left when the fruit is removed.

But I'm not making excuses.

This room they've put me in. At first, I thought I didn't deserve it. Not for the reasons you think. It contains all the things I'd ever wanted in my non-parental life, a huge library, a desk, top of the range laptop – with Word, not Pages, a printer that worked, a window overlooking the sea, coffee that never got cold on tap by day, cava by night! This all seemed more like Heaven than Hell's waiting room. I didn't deserve it and I couldn't understand why I had been given any of it, not at the time.

I spent a good three days enjoying the luxuries, almost perversely forgetting what I'd done. Until one by one, they began to go wrong. The e key stopped working on the laptop, which is why I've written them in, and the printer doesn't hold much ink. Not sure how long it's got, to be honest. It's hellishly annoying.

I was soon no longer able to taste the coffee and the cava had no effect on me whatsoever – and I'd been using that to dull a certain pain.

The books' pages (every book on all the TBR piles in the world) turned to ash as I opened them. Tiny puffs of light, and then darkness as each one extinguished in a phoenix-like flurry of flame.

Whatever there is here is magic, because I feel as light in my mind as I did in my twenties, before childbirth nearly killed me twice and I embraced the dark cave of my mind. I don't have the indulgence of depression now, only deep, irrevocable sadness. All the time. Trust me, it's worse.

All the things you wanted in your non-parental life, just out of reach. You can neither have nor keep them, yet there they are, day in, day out, these last five years taunting and tantalizing my soul.

I do deserve that.

I'd like to tell you how hard it was for me, motherhood. How suffocating. Depression is a cavern with an octopus living inside. Sometimes you get to play on the shore and feel the sun on your face, and those are good days. On the best days, you get to take a dingy out onto the water – those are the days where you forget.

On other days though, there's a shadow casting a net over the bay, chilled and slick tendrils draw you back into the cold cave with ease. You can be in there cradling the creature with twenty others around you, and not hear a single one of them.

I had problems. I thought I was getting better, but it seems I wasn't made for motherhood – too selfish. I couldn't even kill myself. I just sat there. Til my husband came home. Can you imagine finding that? It seems I'd even made a coffee and drunk it with blood-stained hands. I suppose it would've been hot. What was it I said?

'I had to get them before they got me.'

Those little balls of starlight! What did I have to fear from them?

I think it was a neighbour who called the police in the end.

Maybe it stemmed from my own chaotic childhood. I remember almost pushing my alcoholic mother down the stairs when I was 15. I was trying to get my younger brother, whom I was bringing up, ready for football training. She'd just hit me over the head with an empty Vodka bottle, disturbing an old wound, how gauche! My father, bless him, was working three jobs and I nearly killed her that night. If she'd gone down, she'd have gone right down. I was present then too and able to take a few deep breaths. Cancer did the work for me, some time later. I honestly thought the monkey was off my back.

I'm selfish. I've had time to think about this.

But I'm not making any excuses.

If you are reading this, please understand, I don't want your pity. I don't deserve it. I only crave your hate, that's where I bathe now.

I just wanted, while I still could, to tell the story of what happened to my little girls, because I can feel a change here. The walls are closing in and the room isn't as big as it was when I first arrived. It's definitely contracting, the way the walls in the halls do. Not that I visit them often, but the few times I've passed through, I've noticed that. You must yourself have come through them. I wonder how narrow they are now.

I know that I deserve this. No excuses shall be made here.

There is nothing more evil than killing your own children.

I want it noted that I was a prisoner long before this ever came to pass, all parents are, in one way or another, but that's no excuse. I hadn't realised at the time that it was an open prison and I had everything. I was blind. I want others to see... me, for what I am, and also how lucky they are. This is why I am so aware now, I think. The building has cleared away all the brain fog so that finally I can see. This truly is Hell. It's not at all what I expected.

Not long now. I hope this printer keeps working. If a thing is worth doing, it's worth doing well.

You'll have seen how many rooms there are. I can only guess, but I imagine that there are all types of people here. I wonder, truly, if I am the worst of them.

Some nights, I can hear the children laughing, just out of reach in the hallway. The way they did in a Premier Inn. Racing to see who can find number 8 or number 20 and who is going to put the key card in the door first. I'm sure some of the rooms they are running to can't be all that safe for little children and they're out there without me. It feels like I'm killing them again.

Sometimes James is here. I try to close my mind to the look on his face. I can't even describe it. Confusion, terror, fear, hate, sadness and desolation: is there a name for the look that contorts all those into one? The building won't let me look away though, the more I close him off, the more I see him. The pictures on the walls take on his face, so too, the reflections in the window. I see him when I look at my own self in the mirror. It's best to keep him, where he lives, in the corner of my eye, never gone but never fully there either.

I've gotten used to it, kind of.

My fear now is what comes next here. There is definitely change afoot here. Is this actually a waiting room in purgatory before the fire that I did expect, or much, much worse? Think about the worst thing you can imagine... Your brain stops you, right? Mine does not. There is nothing more existential than the dread of waking from a short nap. The feeling intensifies every day.

But I don't want your sympathy.

I've never made any excuses. Even in the dock at court. My lawyer told me to blame James.

'Not there for me, never home, not interested,' that wasn't the truth, everyone has their cross to bear. No-one deserves what I did.

Diminished responsibility due to mental instability. No. Not that. I've always had to be strong, except that one time. I wasn't making any excuses. I can own it. This lack of an e key could drive you to murder before James ever could.

If there was one thing I wasn't expecting, it was for James to kill me. I bled to death right there on

the pavement in front of the High Court and the
second to last thought to race through my head was
that I'd killed four people that day. And then I saw
my children's faces. I, who had never believed in
heaven in the first place, knew I'd never see them
there as my blood pooled under me.

Not that I would've deserved it.

Poor wee things would still've been happy to see
me, such is the umbilical bond.

I didn't believe in Hell, either, then.

Ironically, I've had so much time since I've been
here. You feel a presence, but don't see a soul.

I might be writing this for nothing. Maybe no-
one will ever see it or care for my words of evil.

Late last night, something woke me. For a
change, it wasn't a dream about James or the girls,
it was a dream about you. Whenever or whomever
you are.

If you're reading this, you must be free to roam
and investigate or discover. What is it like to read
the thoughts of the evil? Do you think I am evil? For
my part, I am sorry to have put you through it. I
take no pleasure in sharing the darkness of the
innermost corners of my mind. I think I have been
quite thoughtful. I could've described the sitting
room better. Who knew such small bodies held so
much blood? I didn't like to see the baby dolls in
their cot either, the blanket granny had knitted

oozing on top of them and the brain matter on the floor like loose noodles.

I try not to think about it, but as I've said, it's impossible to forget here. The more I think about you, in the liminal space between sleeping and waking, the more I wonder, what was it, that brought you here? To have your hands on these pages you must be free, mustn't you? But then I wonder... how nosy, vain and disturbed would you need to be to want to read them, what is it that has drawn you into this dark Hell?

Maybe you aren't real at all. Maybe you aren't even reading it. Maybe you are the one glimmer of light in all this darkness and I simply made you up as a writer would, even one who writes for no-one. I doubt it though. This building hasn't let me have a thought of my own since I arrived here. Why would it start with you?

No. No. I want you to consider how free you are. How long have you been here? Day 4 or day 4044? Could you freely tell this tale to someone else or has something struck you dumb? Please, think. I can't tell if you are an opportunity, a glitch in the routine for a reason or the Boss of Hell level 4. But either way...you've shown up here, if you have. And you're reading, if you are. I'd love to know why. Are you as imprisoned as the rest of us?

I've been blind and now I can see. Now I can see more than I expected to, before I was evil, I was a glass-half-full, silver linings type of gal. So maybe you are here for a reason.

Maybe I am. Maybe it wasn't all for nothing? I have to believe that. Wake up! Whatever it is keeping you here. Loosen the shit out of it. Stop reading this and move on. Think of me like Jacob Marley… I always did have a good imagination and a natty way of wearing a scarf. It can't be a good thing you're here.

I'm going to sign off now. I'm tired, so tired. I have the strangest feeling I won't have to wait much longer to see what the next chapter of Hell is going to bring.

I am so sorry for what I've done and wish I could take it back. I am sorry I was blind, I am sorry I was weak, I am sorry I was selfish. I am sorry.

But, as I've said before. I'm not making any excuses.

Brayden blinked and shuffled through the pages to see if he had missed one. Susurrations that had begun like a draft across an imperfectly-closed window had gotten louder as he read this last page, sounding more like whispers, or echoes of something more sinister. The pages rattled in his hand. The woman was mental, obviously. This room was some kind of cell.

Her feeling of entrapment was getting to him. He almost thought the walls were closing in, just as she had described. He stood on shaky legs. He had no stomach for these psychological games. They didn't scare him. He was just... ready to move on. It must be getting late. Time to see what was waiting on the next floor. He set his foot on the first step, took a deep breath, and went up.

Brayden was brought up short at the top of the stairs by the sight of an emaciated man standing in the hallway. He was bald but for a ring of dirty white wisps of hair circling his crown. His ash-grey skin was bare except for a filthy loincloth. His sunken rib cage was accentuated by his distended belly, which in turn stood in marked contrast to spindly, bone-thin legs.

As Brayden moved reluctantly closer, he could see the man's face was gaunt. The eye socket he could see looked freshly empty, still bloody enough for the man to dip a finger in and go back to writing on the wall.

Brayden braced a hand against the wall and fought the waves of nausea that threatened to overtake him as the man's hand neared the grotesque inkwell again.

A gag escaped Brayden's throat, and the man turned.

"Mama," the man said. "Oh, Mama." Then he turned and fled, surprisingly sprightly, disappearing into the shadows at the end of the hall.

Brayden raised his flask and took a look pull. He read the words the man had left and nodded wearily before approaching the door.

Untitled

Jae Margal

Quick—
Feed it those feverish souls
Full of despair
Call to it
In your shaky whisper
Hear the damned beat the slab
In the lobe hoary halls
Of the dead
Curse these hellish demons
Doomed in the Hyperion
Foolish shadows
Dance beneath a hallowed flame
Hush now
The dead are already tamed

8. Replacement

Jaime Bree

A shaft of light appeared through the shallow gap under the door, flickering in unison with a staticky pulsating sound.

A definitive 'ting tinging' accompanied the noise.

Was it a bell? Like one of those ignorant service types, calling a servant to heel, or the distant chime of a grandfather clock counting the hour? An air of nostalgic charm wrapped in a sinister history?

Whatever it was it soon dissipated into the mutterings of a male voice.

The light, once determined and aware of its trajectory, now faced interruption as the muttering man started to shuffle across the floor. His shadow paced to and fro, accompanying the flickering and pulsating in perfect harmony.

Proclamations inaudible, but definitely proclaiming something, in loud nonsensical whispers, while he moved like Newton's cradle close to the door. Hypnotic and far too easy to lose yourself in his momentum. Back and forth, back and forth. To-ing and fro-ing. Whispering and muttering, pacing and shuffling.

Brayden stepped forward, inquisitive, wanting to hear the words more clearly. The floorboards creaked underfoot.

The man stopped at the noise.

Brayden leaned in, ever so slowly, holding his breath.

A silent stand-off. Two men, either side of a door.

The other man giggled. Desperately trying to suppress it at first, but struggling to do so. The giggle escaped and became a laugh, growing in volume. Unrefined and loutish, like he couldn't help himself, like he'd die if he didn't let it out, like he wasn't of sound mind, like a psychotic, maniacal freak, ready to kill.

His fist slammed the door.

Brayden jumped back.

Another slam. Harder.

The laughter returned to a giggle, then to a quiet, childlike sob. A muffled, snivelling, attention-seeking sob. It went on and on. Deviously realistic, worryingly eerie. As the man sobbed, the light inside the room increased, seeped out of every crack in the door, every avenue it could find into the hallway, as if his mock misery controlled the intensity of it. The pulsing and static were now so chaotic, they caused the door to rattle on its hinges.

Brayden took another step back, half expecting it to burst open with some sort of furore or confrontation. A high-pitched, uncomfortable whine permeated the air for a brief second, for just enough time to make Brayden bend double, covering his ears.

Then... dark.

Silence.

'So?' The man's voice asked.

Brayden raised his eyes to the door that was now standing open.

'Are you coming in?'

Brayden didn't move. He remained looking into the darkened room.

'You'll enter soon enough,' the man said, 'But if you're staying out there...' Out of the darkness and into the corridor slid a solid wooden chair. It positioned itself perfectly in the doorway looking into the room. 'You might want to sit.'

Brayden was once again unmoving.

'Seek and you will find. Pay no heed to what's on your mind,' the man's voice whispered. He then broke into a deliberate, mocking laugh. 'You scared of the dark, boy?'

And at that exact moment, the light flicked on, and there he was, standing in the doorway, naked apart from a dirty, ripped pair of knee-length shorts. His appearance would have unnerved even the most stoic. Gaunt, withered and emaciated, it was incredible that his fragile frame could remain upright. He looked like he'd been on a heroin-fuelled binge for half a century, but what really stood out were the tattoos. Every inch of his body was covered in graffiti-style tags, faded and wrinkled, and covering a multitude of scars.

He waited. He knew Brayden would sit, and when he did, a smile crossed his face, so wide it showed his deteriorating teeth.

'And now I have your attention,' he went on, and held out his bony hand to shake. 'Go on, beautiful idiot. I don't bite. Not yet, anyway.' Another beaming grin appeared as Brayden took the man's hand in his and shook it.

'I'm Seth,' he said, 'And I guarantee you won't leave this place the same as you came in.' He pulled up a chair. An exact copy of the one Brayden sat on, right down to the peeling paint and the cracks in the wood. And now the stand-off was a sit-off. A seated man in a corridor facing a seated man just inside a room.

'I'm guessing you have a lot of questions, so I'll make it easy for you. I'll tell you why I'm here and then you can reciprocate and tell me why you are. It's not a question of agreeing, by the way, it's a question of you knowing this is the deal.'

He leaned back in the chair, smirking arrogantly as the wood creaked beneath him.

'You see, I want you to be scared of me, to not want to be here. I want you to feel uneasy to the point of distraction, to the point of a deep-felt thronging in the pit of your stomach that tells you, confirms to you, that you should never have stepped foot in this building, and cements in your mind that leaving is more than likely not an option.'

Seth leaned forward, another teeth-bearing smile covering his face.

'Or...'

A deliberate pause, taking in Brayden's demeanour – assessing, manipulating the moment.

'I could be bluffing.'

He continued leaning forward, staring directly into Brayden's eyes, losing himself deep in them. In his head, he left the chair, peeled back Brayden's intense blue pupils like a door and climbed into his mind, smirking and deciphering his racing thoughts.

Then he slowly leant back in his chair, pleased with the discomfort he was causing, but never once dropping his stare. Waiting, testing, counting the minutes before Brayden looked away.

'Not bad,' he said, 'You've lasted longer than most. You have strength. That's good. I hate a pushover. There's absolutely no fun when they are whimpering and pathetic. Takes all the sense of adventure out of the moment, and that would, in no uncertain terms, spoil my day. We can't have that, can we? *I* can't have that.'

He slammed his fist against the door frame so hard it splintered, leaving his blood smeared on it.

'I won't have that,' he shouted. The words echoed down the corridor, pummelled the walls and rebounded off the doors. Shouts of obscenities from within the building echoed back towards them. Seth smiled.

'They hate me, loathe me. *I* loathe me. You'll loathe me by the time we're done here. You'll pity me too when you realise, but it'll be too late, and then you'll just feel regret and embarrassment at how unbelievably stupid you've been, how easily tricked you were and how blind you are.'

He pulled a small knife from the pocket of his shorts, stabbed it into the arm of the chair, slowly, rhythmically at first.

'I wasn't always like this. I was once sophisticated and confident. None of these tattoos on my skin. I was perfect boyfriend material. Perfect management material. Perfect friend material.'

He began to stab the knife harder, quicker, more aggressively.

'So, why didn't they see me?' And then he embedded it with one last severe stab into the wood. His hand remained gripped around the handle as he continued.

'I talked to them. They didn't see me. Approached them. Nothing. I shouted in their small, pathetic faces. They wouldn't hear me. I threatened. I stole. I abused. I even told jokes. They refused to look at me. "I'm right here," I'd scream, I'd threaten. But, still, they wouldn't see me. I was made to feel small, insignificant, unappreciated for who I was, what I was. Ignored. And slowly, over time as I looked in mirrors, I couldn't see me either. I was being reduced to nothing. I became nothing.'

A tear rolled onto Seth's cheek, sat there for a brief moment, then burnt into his skin. A moment of weakness incarcerated among myriad tattoo-covered scars. His grip on the handle of the knife intensified. He squeezed so hard, his whitened knuckles almost broke from his skin, then he pulled the knife from the wood in one go. Weak as he looked, he was supremely strong, and Brayden sat paralysed with fear.

Seth placed his finger onto the tip of the blade and spun it. It cut into his skin. Blood dripped from the wound, but he didn't seem to notice or care. He then ran the blade flat over one arm, then the other, then his chest.

'You like my tattoos? They literally tell the story of my life, but don't look at the surface of a person, my friend. Look at what lies beneath.'

He pushed the blade into his skin around the blackened edge of one of the graffiti tags, like he was cutting around a cake stuck to the side of a tin.

'This one for instance...' he paused, deep in thought. 'This absolute son of a bitch, this...' The words hissed from his mouth, momentarily leaving him speechless. It was as if finishing the sentence would cause him considerable pain. It took a moment to compose himself.

'Well, let's just say, many aren't deserved, but this one...' And then he lifted the perfectly cut piece of skin up to reveal his flesh underneath. It moved and writhed, like it was its own entity, but what was even more bizarre was the noise. Screams of terror and anguish so desperate, so disturbing, they would haunt anyone for the rest of their lives.

'I like bringing this motherfucker out. Let him know he's not forgotten. Remind him of where he is and what I did to shut down his vile, insidious arrogance. He learnt quickly, oh so quickly, and he was a joy to defeat.'

Seth slowly moved the skin back into place.

'I took from him what he loved the most. To hate. And I enjoyed every single minute of it.'

He paused. 'And now what's his is mine.'

He smiled, covering the newly-opened wound with his hand. He closed his eyes, took a breath. One long, deep, contented breath, and when he took his hand away, the tattoo and the scar were gone.

'What a relief it is to be able to tell someone, to confess to someone what I did. To off-load the burden. A problem shared and all that.'

He sighed again and with each, elated, almost orgasmic sigh, more tattoos and scars faded and cleared.

'To have a man take your hand, welcome you to talk, help alleviate the pain with his gesture of friendship.'

His tattoos were now almost completely gone, leaving his skin smooth and scar-free.

'And that was your first, unbelievably stupid mistake. Don't you know you never shake a stranger's hand in here?'

Out of the corner of his eye, Brayden could see something appearing on his right hand. A drawing of sorts, an invisible needle reproducing the tattoos that had faded from Seth's hand. Brayden quickly pulled up his sleeve. His arm was also covered. He rolled up his trousers to reveal more tattoos.

'Your strength, whilst worth applauding, is clearly out-matched by your lack of common sense.'

Brayden tore off his shirt. He was covered in the exact tattoos, the exact scars that had just left Seth's body.

'And now, it's your turn...'

Brayden looked at him with desperate eyes, still trying to take in his scarred appearance. He felt numb.

'...to say why you're here,' Seth clarified. 'Do you even know where you are?'

Brayden slowly looked around. His eyes widened as realisation dawned. A seated man in a corridor facing a seated man inside a room. But he was no longer the man in the corridor, he was sitting just inside the room, looking out. The blood-stained door frame surrounded him perfectly. He stared at Seth, sitting where he had sat, wearing what he had worn, becoming him.

Brayden slowly looked down. His body, covered in tattoos, faded and wrinkled, covered in a multitude of scars, was emaciated and thin, like he'd been on a heroin-fuelled binge for half a century. He was wearing a dirty, ripped pair of knee-length shorts. He could feel something pressing on his leg from the pocket. He placed his hand inside and pulled out the knife.

'Enjoy your time here. Let's hope the next visitor to the building decides to shake hands, too.'

Seth stood up, kicked the chair back into the room. Brayden ducked as it ricocheted off the door frame above his head. When he sat back up, he was staring at a perfect replica of himself, smiling, fixing his collar, flattening his hair with his hand.

The door slammed, accompanied by his piercing, desperate scream as an intense light seeped out of every crack, throbbing into the hallway. Slowly it dissipated, until only a shaft of light appeared through the shallow gap under the door, flickering in unison with a staticky, pulsating sound accompanied by the mutterings of a male voice.

Brayden ran. And kept running. To the stairs and up, up to whatever the next floor had in store for him and *away* from psycho tattooed guys. His skin still crawled and stung in several of the places where he had seen – or thought he saw – the tags appear.

"Whatchu' got?!" Brayden demanded, coming off the top without slowing. He was ready to charge something gross and creepy, even if it got fake pus all over him, just to *prove* that none of this was real.

The hallway stood quiet and empty. Brayden slowed, suspicious that a surprise still lurked for him somewhere.

"You won't win," he called. "This place won't win! I'm no coward." After a moment, he read the words on the wall, neatly stenciled in black paint this time. The fading adrenaline in his system left him shaky.

"You won't win," he muttered again. And since there was no knocker, or even doorknob, on the door, he pushed it open and stepped in.

Untitled
Mila H.

Come tear me away from this mystical landmark

curious inhibitions left dark calling unfettered

Somewhere the hallows of these walls marked
innocents for death

souls festered between living and aftermath of
sustenance

Hell squandered even its own residents

Now awaits the accumulation of more human prey

Meet him majestically in this building of doom

The escalator bell heralds the death knell of the
Devil

Demons fly between floors scurrying the
damnation of lifeblood

Windows now blinded to the exposure of evil

Stories high as cowardice trembled in fear

No one to save or rescue

where is my saviour

prayers unanswered

Hell hold me not close and let the scourge of
purgatory intervene to help my last days pass with
a glimmer of the sun

nor burning hot red but comforting yellow...

9. The Sin-eater of Cumberland Knob

Suzanna Lundale

Suzanna Lundale

Author's Historical Note

The practice of sin-eating came to the Appalachian Mountains with colonists from Britain, especially Wales and the Welsh Marches, Scotland, and Ireland. Very little solid historical evidence exists about the practice and the people who performed it, though it seems to have been practiced largely in the 17th and 18th centuries. In at least some isolated areas of Appalachia, the practice survived longer still. Modern-day Appalachian conjure man Jake Richards reports having witnessed the practice in North Carolina during his childhood in the 1980's. This author and historian is by no means finished researching this fascinating and elusive topic, but for the present tale, we will have to accept that some conjecture has been applied to enable the telling of it.

Those caveats presented, what can be said is that the sin-eater tended to be the poorest of the poor, a person reviled and ostracized for their unclean state, but nonetheless needed by communities who believed quite literally in the eternal danger to the souls of their loved ones should they go forth from this world burdened by the weight of sin. Thus, the sin-eater was called and served a ritual meal, generally bread with beer or ale, which was consumed over the body, ritually transferring the sins of the departed to the sin-eater. The sin-eater was paid a nominal sum and urged to go as far and as fast as possible, so long as he was within summoning distance when next the community needed his services.

Brayden came to the door at the end of the hall and found it ajar. With a shuddering look down the hallway he'd just passed through, he pushed the door open and went in. Experiences on previous floors had prepared him well enough that he was little surprised to find himself in a wooden hovel, unadorned. As he entered, a simple rocking chair appeared, which he settled into with a shrug. He looked around for clues, but found very little. The place was beyond spartan. Just poor, airless, and redolent of unwashed body. Disgusting.

"Might as well wipe that sneer off your face," growled a voice. Brayden turned his head sharply and saw a... man? A person, weathered and withered, sitting cross-legged on the floor. "You think you're better than me?" The creature lapsed into a long, ragged coughing fit before finally continuing, his voice clearer, and sounding more... educated than Brayden expected. "Because you've never been poor, you think I don't smell the stink of sin on you?"

Brayden chuckled. "I don't really go in for that, uh, stink of sin stuff, so I think I'm okay."

He thought his host was coughing again, but what emerged was a chilling dry laugh. When he spoke, it was with a different voice, a woman's voice – not like a man imitating a woman, but an actual woman – with a honeyed timbre, and a lilt of accent Brayden couldn't place. "Oh, he doesn't go in for it. Well, that's all right then, isn't it?" Her tone was mocking.

Brayden looked around the hovel for where the ventriloquist might be hiding.

"Stop looking for hidden ladies and pay attention," said the creature in the male voice again. "Every newcomer gets the story just once. Sort of a *contractual obligation,* you might say." From the folds of his rags, the man pulled out a battered pipe and began to suck on it unlit.

"I was born to a good family when these mountains still rang with the accents of the Old Country, though the War for American Independence was well over with. My father had made a lot of money in shipping, and brought the money, and his new bride, up into the mountains to establish himself. I was the firstborn son, named after my father, but I... haven't used that name for a long while. I had a brother, George, and three sisters, Ida, Helen, and Margaret."

Brayden sat forward. "Why don't you use that name? What name *do* you use, then?"

"You can call me Old Hob. I'll get to the other part later," he answered between coughs. "Now, where was I? Oh, yes. I was the eldest son, and I was a complete wastrel. I never met a strong drink I didn't want to make my own, and I got into scrapes and debts on both sides of the mountain. My father despaired of ever seeing me settle and take his place at the head of the family. My mother had a sweet spot for me, but even she couldn't cover for everything."

Brayden thought fleetingly of his own mother, always making excuses for him, always pretending he was something he wasn't. *Foolish woman.*

"So that day," Old Hob was saying, "I saw my childhood friend, Nathaniel, approaching the house dressed like a lord, riding his father's favorite stallion. I was sulking around after an argument with Father and invited him to join me for a drink. 'Not I,' says he. 'I'm on my way to ask your father for Ida's hand.'

"Of course, then I *insisted* that we drink the health of my sister and her almost-betrothed. I threatened to tell Father about how Nathaniel once chose a whore for her resemblance to my sister if he insulted me by refusing to have one friendly drink with me. Didn't matter that he'd never touched a whore in his life. Father would have believed it, at least enough to put an end to the courtship. So he settled his fancy self on a tree stump, and together we drank to his future with Ida at his side.

"Then Nathaniel brushed himself down and headed up to the house to get the thing done, while I went off to rest up from the excitement against a favorite tree. Say, I don't suppose you have any drink with you?"

Brayden, immersed in the tale, started back to the hovel. He pulled out his flask and tossed it to his host, who took a long pull, then spat on the floor. "What the fuck?" demanded Brayden.

"We are not allowed strong drink," said the woman's voice primly from Old Hob's mouth. "Not even for *this* story. *Especially* for this story."

"How do y–" Brayden started to ask, now wondering if Old Hob was managing to make the woman's voice himself.

"Wait a bit," said Old Hob wearily. "Let me finish this part. I might as well tell you now that Nathaniel and I had also drunk the health of my future nieces and nephews. Each one, individually. When he got to the house, he was admitted by Ida herself, flushed and excited. She ushered him in to see Father and went to make sure refreshments were ready for a dignified celebration at the conclusion of the conversation. I suppose she must have smelled the alcohol, or maybe she was too excited." Old Hob curled into a paroxysm of coughing that stretched on a few minutes, at least.

"My father," he continued drily, "was not nearly so excited. He was offended and enraged that this young man had come before him *inebriated* to ask for Ida's hand in marriage. He said the Lord had protected the family that day, by showing Nathaniel's unsuspected true nature. He sent him away and promised to shoot him if he ever set foot on the property again. Ida's sobs could be heard as the door closed behind him."

"But it was your fault," protested Brayden. "That doesn't seem fair."

"Oooh, fair, he wants," said a deep voice from Old Hob's mouth. *Not just the one extra voice,* thought Brayden. *Cool trick.* "Will he think the next part is fair, Old Hob? Do you think he will?"

"Let me finish," said Old Hob in his own reedy voice. "I'm almost there. Nathaniel was less cowed and more angered by my father's rejection. He tried to find me to hatch a plan together, but I was already tucked against a favorite tree, sleeping. So he hatched a plan himself. He decided to wait until nightfall and set a small fire in an outbuilding. He would rush in and put the fire out, protecting my father's property and my family. Then my father would have no choice but to accept Nathaniel's request with his blessing. It didn't occur to him that he would never be able to explain how he was still so near at that late hour."

Brayden grimaced sympathetically at the disaster he knew must follow.

"Yes, you see it. Any man in his right mind would. We had had a dry summer. The family was all abed by the time it started. The fire spread fast, especially after it hit the barrel of lamp oil stored in the tack area of the stable. The explosion probably woke some of them, as it woke me out in the woods, but it was too late. They all slept upstairs.

By the time I roused and got there, flames had engulfed the house. I tried to get inside, to get to them – either to save them or die with them. Either one. But burned beams blocked the doors. I could only stand and watch my world disappear, trapped outside." Old Hob dissolved again into what Brayden now recognized as a smoky cough.

"And they blamed you." It was a statement. Brayden didn't have to ask. He could see it. The disgraced drunk son, found outside a house burned by probable arson.

"They blamed me. Figured Father had cut me out of the business in favor of my brother, George, as everyone expected him to. Figured I'd set the fire in retaliation."

"And Nathaniel didn't say a word," Brayden guessed.

"Not a word. He knew if he spoke up and admitted to it, he'd be hanged. He brought me food sometimes, for a little while, out of guilt, though he never told me what he had done. I still thought it was a horrible accident. Some candle ember smoldering in a corner after a servant locked the horses in or something."

"If Nathaniel would have been hanged, why weren't you?"

"They thought about it, to be sure. I was locked up for a time. Some folk had enough doubt from my denials, and some thought it was a better punishment to let me starve to death on my own family's land. In the end, the judge decided not to trouble the hangman and let me go. I was *encouraged* to give up my right of inheritance in favor of a cousin, and I was allowed to stay on the land, in the wild part.

By late-October, my miserable forestcraft wasn't up to keeping me alive in the open any longer. I built myself this little hovel here." He tapped the floor he sat on almost fondly. "But the small game disappeared pretty soon after. I didn't have what you'd call *winter provisions*. I hadn't been able to get properly drunk for many weeks by that point. Every night, I fell asleep hoping not to wake up."

"But you kept waking up," prompted Brayden.

"I kept waking up. I thought that was my punishment, for disappointing my parents, for not dying with my family. I kept waking up. Cold, hungry, miserable, and alone."

"I feel an 'until' coming."

"Of course, there's an 'until' coming. Wouldn't be much of a story, otherwise." Old Hob struggled to wrestle his cough under control. "*Until* our nearest neighbor, Jed McClure, died."

"He left you money?"

"No, boy. He left me sins. You see, in the Old Country, people used to have sin-eaters come to take on the sins of people who died unshriven, because a lot of places didn't have their own priest to get there in time to administer Last Rites. The people who settled in these mountains brought that notion with them, and these mountains are *full* of folk who don't have a priest or what have you nearby."

"How does someone 'take on' the sins of dead people? You don't mean they eat part of the dead person, do you? That would be crazy gross."

"No," Old Hob sighed, "nothing like that. The sin-eater takes a ritual meal of bread and beer, which he consumes over the corpse. He gets paid a nominal fee and consumes this ritual meal, and then he leaves as soon as possible."

"And you ate this Jed guy's sins? Wasn't there competition for that?"

"I was fortunate, if you call it that. The night he died, a cold rain fell. There were patches of ice on the road, and especially on the bridge the nearest sin-eater would have to cross. They were desperate to get him into the ground before a hard freeze. I hadn't eaten in days, and I knew the family was worried, so I agreed to do it as a one-time thing. The McClures had been some of the few people to speak up for me after the fire. It seemed like the right thing to do. The widow was so grateful, she gave me a loaf of bread and a jug of beer to take with me after. I finished both that night and got violently sick because my body wasn't prepared for it. At least Jed's sins weren't heavy."

"It was a kind thing you did," said the deep voice. "And my biggest sin was not fighting harder for you after that fire."

Old Hob patted his own leg gently, as if consoling himself. "You did what you could," he said in his own voice.

"Wait, so these voices... these other voices you do... They're people whose sins you ate?" asked Brayden. He was on the edge of his seat now, excited to have an answer to the mystery.

"Oh yes," said the woman's voice. "He carries a part of every one of us."

"How many people did you do this for?"

"I don't know. Many..."

"How old were you when you came here?"

"I had just turned eighteen when I started. They called me Hob. Said I didn't have a right to use the name my father gave me. I probably hadn't seen 30 winters when Hob became Old Hob. Living that rough ages a man. And the sins aged me, too, some of them. I don't suppose I was past 35 when I came here."

"What do you mean 'some of' the sins aged you? Do they have different potency, if they're worse?" Brayden's eyes sparkled with professional interest, his fingers reflexively dropping to his notched belt.

"Yes, people like Jed, they have the lighter sins – maybe he took the Lord's name in vain when he stubbed his toe, maybe he pretended not to be home one time when a poor relation came asking for money yet again, that kind of thing. Those sins, you don't really feel."

"What about the other ones? What were those like?" Brayden leaned forward.

"They varied, too. The spring after it started, a... man died. I will not speak his name. He was a pillar of the community, God-fearing man, always ready to help people in need... but that man had dark secrets. He and his wife had taken in a number of orphans. They didn't adopt them as their own, but raised them and trained them with skills, so they could make their way in the world. They never asked for anything from them in return. At least, not officially. It turned out that man enjoyed inflicting pain. Liked seeing how long a person – boy or girl – could hold out against even the most humiliating requests, when subjected to pain."

Old Hob was cut off by convulsive heaving, though Brayden didn't think there was anything inside to come up.

"They were lucky that we took them in! Blessed," asserted a pinched male voice. "Those orphans were nothing, alone, forsaken in the eyes of man and God! And I extended grace to them. I brought them into a Christian household. I fed them and taught them. They owed me that little assistance with my... experiments."

Brayden guffawed. "Experiments! I like that. Did you tell the kids how lucky they were? What do you think they hated more? When you beat them, or when you shoved your–"

As he spoke, in an instant, Old Hob's body was suddenly and completely suffused by flames. Brayden blinked, and the flames were gone, leaving the body instead covered with burns in various stages of healing and infection. Even as a strangled cry escaped Brayden's throat, he saw his host returned to his original dishevelment. *Hallucination? What the fuck?*

When Old Hob spoke again, it was as the nameless tormentor, shouting, "Enough! I was a Godly man! They were nothing. They were as the beasts in the field. Mine to do with as I saw fit! I was their shepherd, their master!" He was interrupted by coughing that racked his whole body.

"So you see," shuddered Old Hob, back in control of his voice, "Some sins were far heavier. I aged decades the night I took on that man's sins. I could barely stagger back here. That was one of the worst."

"One of the worst?" Brayden asked. Far from disgusted by the unnamed dead man's sins, Brayden's mind danced with prurient ideas and questions he knew would not be answered if he asked them. "There were worse than that?"

Old Hob looked up sharply. "Ah, that's right. Sometimes I get so carried away talking to another person, I forget why you're here."

Brayden scowled at this stinking shade who took a superior tone with him. *How dare he?* "Why I'm here? I'm here to explore. I'm going to be the first person to give people the scoop about this place. I'm going to be set for life."

"I think we're almost done here. But there is one last tale to share."

"Another perv?"

"I suppose that's short for 'pervert,' but I'm going to have to disappoint you. No, the last tale came when my old friend, Nathaniel, who had found another wealthy and lovely girl to marry, had too much to drink in celebration of the birth of his son, the fifth child his patient wife had presented him with, but the first to carry the crucial organ for carrying on the family name. On his way home from celebrating, he got lost in the darkening woods. At some point, he fell off his horse – that horse was fine-looking, but a famous coward. Probably, he heard an owl and got spooked. The horse was standing outside the stable in the morning, Nathaniel still dangling from one stirrup, stone dead."

Brayden sat back, losing interest in the sad little ending. "That was it? He just fell off his horse?"

"That was it," Old Hob wheezed. He punched his chest feebly. "That was it for both of us, in a way. They called me in, gave me my fee, my bread and beer. I was sad to see my friend gone in his prime. I was also sad because being there, in the parlor of his house... it just all reminded me of what my life might have been. So I leaned over his body, and started the ritual meal... And then I knew, as if it were a memory. I knew his greatest sins – setting the fire, first, and just behind it, letting me take the blame. Letting me become," he struggled to his feet and gestured down at his broken form, "this. My dearest friend had done that."

"Come on," scoffed Brayden. "You really never knew? You never suspected?"

"Never," replied Old Hob. "I never even suspected, until I knew, all at once. I think I screamed, still bent over the traitor's body. Someone hustled me out. Perhaps they remembered that I had once been the boy who was Nathaniel's closest friend. Perhaps they simply thought that even sins as light as they supposed his to be had proven too much, that I was filled to capacity and could hold no more. I don't know what they thought. I don't care. I staggered through the woods to my family's land. Saw it in my mind as it had been that hateful day, with the addition of Nathaniel's form skulking in every shadow." He was silent so long, Brayden started to rise, but Old Hob stayed him with a raised hand.

"A few days later, my cousin's boys found my body floating in the creek Nathaniel and I had played in as boys. They thought I'd slipped and fallen in, though I'm sure there were other theories. And then I woke up, and I was here. Alone forever except for the echoes of my fellow sinners, and the occasional newcomer, like you."

Behind Brayden, the door creaked open. Old Hob waved him toward it.

"I've fulfilled my obligation. Go, explore your new home. Find a place to unpack your own sack of sins for future... *explorers.*"

Brayden walked out the door and back down the hall toward the stairs. He moved slowly, as if underwater, his senses dull. He was *tired*.

With every step up, he emerged a little more from his torpor, back to normal, and past it, his heart speeding. His breathing grew shallow. Stars danced before his eyes. He clung to the stair rail against the vertigo.

A shuffling chuckle at the edge of his hearing grew in strength and volume until it was a wild cacophony of voices surrounded him. His own accompanying laugh started out weak and led, as he dropped to his knees, to a howling cackle that finished, just as suddenly, with a scream.

Brayden slumped to the floor, screaming, trapping the sound in the fetal cocoon of his crumbling sanity. He lay there for long minutes after the laughter and screaming faded away.

Eventually, the tears dried.

Eventually, his breathing became even.

Eventually, his fingers ceased their desperate dance over the notches on his belt.

Shakily, Brayden pushed himself onto his knees to read the words pulsing on the wall. He forced himself to his feet. "Almost done," he murmured. "You can do this."

I Don't Deserve This
Teresa Berkowitz

I made them. They were my blood and flesh. They belonged to me.

Little tortures.

Torture is probably too strong of a word. They probably don't even remember.

Fingers grip.
Rope ties.
Pills poison.

Near death isn't death. They cried to each other. They comforted each other. I had to remind them to think of me.

Me. Me. Me.

Why didn't they care about me?

Got out as soon as they could. I died mostly alone. Selfish. So selfish.

Motherhood is divine. Heavenly. I gave them life. Why am I trapped in this suite?

Dark walls
Fingers dig. Pills heal.
Sometimes

.

Redemption can be found in chalk on dark walls and so
I write. When the chalk is gone, I write.

Fingers scrape.
To the bone.

All I wanted was their adoration. And submission.

My only light is the pattern of their lives without me
projected on these dark walls. How happy they are
without me.

Without me.
Without me.

What words will release me?

I write.
Fingers bleed.

10. Room 13

Shawn Morgan

Brayden stared through the open security door leading into the final hallway of the Hyperion residence. The corridor opened up before him as the faint sounds of screams and anguished cries reached him from the rooms below. He noted a single door at the end of the carpeted hallway and walked through until he stood before the entrance to room 13, a grey door with its numerals sitting above the peephole. Taking a deep breath, he reached out and knocked. The door creaked open ever so slightly, swinging inwards away from him.

"Hello?"

The room on the far side of the threshold was dark except for a faint glimmer that caught his eye from somewhere inside. Reaching out, hesitating ever so slightly, he pushed the door the rest of the way open. The pale light from the hallway provided a little more detail to the room, but it largely remained a mystery. His first step was met by a cold chill sliding up his spine, as if warning him of something, but he had not come this far only to turn back, and so continued forward.

"Hello? Mind if I come in? I just want to talk."

A whispering of unintelligible words reached Brayden's ear; teasing, but at the same time beckoning him further inside. The same nagging fear held him still, but a glance back at the hallway reminded him there was not much point in staying if he did not go on. Closing his eyes, he steadied himself, leaning against the frame of the door before nodding and stepping forward.

The room held the same cool feeling he had momentarily felt when the door opened, but this felt more persistent than a simple cool breeze. He reached out to either side of the door, trying to find a light switch, but could find none.

"I know someone's here, but I can't see you. Do you speak? Can you hear me?"

"I'm here."

The voice tickled at his ear, and he felt the presence of someone behind him, but when he spun around, no one was there. He turned back towards the room, but it remained cloaked in darkness, revealing little of what the room housed. As he stepped forward, he heard the unit's door creaking shut behind him, but continued on, not bothering to look back at what he knew he would find.

Brayden reached his arms out, feeling for anything, and was surprised to find a smooth-surfaced wall off to one side that was cool to the touch. As his eyes adjusted to the room's gloom, he noticed a figure standing before him, which sent him stumbling backwards, only to realize that he was, in fact, the mimicking man, dancing backwards away from his own reflection. With his heart hammering in his chest, Brayden exhaled and released a nervous laugh, thinking how goofy he must look.

"Are you the one?"

Brayden spun around to find a man sitting in the center of the room, staring up at him. He sat, largely naked, except for a filthy length of fabric that was wrapped around his body, the remainder of the cloth sitting in a jumbled pile on the floor beside him.

Brayden looked down in confusion. "The one what? Who are you?"

The man sighed and looked away. "I'm Jacob, but no, you are not the one. Merely another." He waved Brayden away like so much trash, unworthy of his time.

"How did you get here? Do you know where you are?"

The man remained motionless on the floor for a time before cocking his head to the side and looking up. "I know where I am," Jacob chuckled as he rolled his neck, staring off into the darkness as if he could see something no one else could. "I know where I am," he continued, "but you wandered in here of your own free will. This is not a place you willingly go on your own."

"What do you know of this place?"

The man continued staring off to the side, so much so that Brayden turned his head, following the man's line of sight, and walked off in that direction. With his hands splayed out before him, he took hesitant steps away from Jacob; the room seemed to lighten with each movement he made, revealing a square room of mirrors, each reflecting back at him, one after another, until he could no longer tell what he was looking at. He turned back towards the center of the room, but found the room empty, save for himself.

"What the hell is going on?"

Turning back to the mirrors, Brayden looked at his reflection and shook his head, but then realized it was not himself he was looking at. Although the clothes were identical, it was Jacob wearing them.

"Are you alright? How did you get in there?"

He reached for the wall, not understanding how the man had moved from behind him to the other side of the mirror, not to mention wearing his clothes. Jacob's lips moved, but no sound permeated the glass wall, leaving Brayden trying to lip-read and guess what the other man was saying. Brayden moved closer to the mirror, but it made no difference.

"I don't know what you're trying to say."

In a flash of movement, Jacob's face burst through the glass, leaving him bleeding profusely. His ravaged flesh framed the rictus of a smile on his face.

"We came here by deeds done or decisions made. I know why I'm here, do you?"

A pair of fists smashed through the glass, grabbing hold of Brayden, as shards of jagged glass sliced into his arms while Jacob pulled him closer to his grinning face.

"Do you know why you're here, Mr. Winchell?" his voice grating from between bleeding split lips, before breaking into hysterical laughs, spraying blood with each wheezing breath. He released

Brayden, who stumbled backwards, away from the wall and the half-emerged figure.

"Because I certainly know why I'm here."

Jacob's voice returned, but this time, it was from the center of the room once more. Brayden scrambled around on all fours, but saw it was the previous version of Jacob sitting before him again. He held up the strip of cloth that he had wrapped around him, as he looked down at his hands.

"A lifetime of ego and malice has led me here."

The cloth in his hands turned from a dirty beige to crimson red, dripping droplets of blood to the floor before the fabric turned to ash in his hands, floating down to the floor with a slow, wafting pace.

Sitting down, Brayden watched the stream of emotions change on Jacob's face from one moment to the next. The man leaned forward, nearly bringing his nose down to the floor, before rocking back up on his heels. He shook as he moved back and forth; a sob built in his throat that threatened to bowl him over until he cried out and rolled forward one last time, disappearing into the floor, like he had never been.

Brayden crawled over to where he had just been, but only the scattered ashes left any indication someone had just been there. He regained his feet and looked around the room; realizing that the light that seemed to emanate from the walls was filling the room with a hazy glow. He followed the path of the mirror walls around the room, his hands tracing their smooth surface with his reflection following him in lock-step.

"Do you know why you're here?"

Brayden spun back, following the sound of the voice, expecting Jacob to be standing there, but he remained alone.

"Where did you go?"

Brayden's voice ricocheted off the walls in echo, but no further sound was made. Turning back the way he had been heading, he set out once more, his hand sliding along the wall.

"Why am I here? That's what you asked?"

He looked up at the ceiling as he continued with a questioning look on his face.

"I heard about this place ages ago. It's the Hyperion, ya' know? The mysterious building that almost no one has been able to get in... and certainly no one has come back out. This place has a reputation. How could I pass that up?"

Reaching the corner of the room opposite where he had entered, Braydon realized there was a gap between the walls. The reflections only gave the impression that the room was a perfect square, when it actually had a passage behind the mirrored wall that was not readily apparent. Stepping around the wall's edge into the hallway left him in a carpeted corridor similar to the hallway outside the apartment.

"What do we have here?"

The hallway led to a pair of doors, the first one slightly ajar. Pulling the door towards him revealed a narrow closet filled with colorful suits and button-up shirts, arranged by shade and hanging from a solitary pole crossing the length of the closet. Along the floor, six pairs of black, wing-tipped dress shoes were lined up, with another six pairs of boots arranged behind them.

"The wardrobe of the man who has it all. The refuge of the man who wants none of it."

The voice reached Braydon's ears from further down the hall, most likely from the second door, he thought. He had waited for the voice (if not the man) to return, so he was not startled by its re-emergence this time. He elbowed the closet door back to its original position and continued down the hallway.

"You have an expensive taste in clothing, Jacob. I know people who would kill for some of what's in there. Bottega Veneta? Moschino? Quite the collection."

As he approached the second door, muffled crying escaped through it. Brayden took a deep breath and opened it, revealing a room that could only be described as an extravagant exercise in room design. Everything from the king-sized sleigh bed weighed down with countless pillows and throw blankets to the oak bookshelf in the far corner, filled with a colorful array of hardcover novels. A fireplace on the left-hand wall housed a blazing log fire, the crackling wood giving off a comforting glow, as if this were a photoshoot for some housekeeping magazine, rather than a bedroom somewhere near the back of the Hyperion.

In the center of the room, Jacob sat amid a mound of blankets pulled from a corner of the bed. Tears glistened on his cheeks as he stared down towards his lap. Brayden stepped into the room, focusing only on the man. As he moved closer, the blanket draped across Jacob's shoulders fell away, revealing another man laying with his head nestled in Jacob's lap, staring blankly at the ceiling as blood dripped from multiple stab wounds onto the blankets around him.

Jacob held a knife above the man, terror and confusion taking turns upon his face as he stared down at his victim.

"What have I done?"

Without a word, Brayden moved closer to him, grabbing the blade from his hand and placing it on a side table, resting against the wall beside the fireplace.

"I couldn't bear to let him go. Leaving for London on a business trip, he said, but I knew differently. I knew once he left, he would never come back. Why couldn't he stay with me? We had a life together; everything we could ever want."

Jacob burst into tears as the figure in his lap disappeared, triggering a reaction within the room that stole the adornments that had made it so beautiful until everything was gone and they were left in a barren chamber, without furniture or decorations.

"This is the price I have to pay. I wanted him to stay, but now he is forever out of my reach."

Jacob looked around at the emptiness he was sentenced to before returning his gaze to Brayden.

"Why would you come here? Don't you understand what this place is?"

A realization dawned on Braydon as he sprinted from the bedroom and down the hall. Into the mirrored room he ran and found the door leading to the hallway open, but where the security door had been was now only a wall. Racing to it, he pressed his hands against the wall, trying to find where the door had disappeared to, but only the wall remained.

Brayden turned back towards Room 13, but found it gone as well. Where the hallway had ended previously, a new L-shaped extension was in place. Down the hall he stumbled, shaking his head as he reached the corner of the corridor and saw a single door waiting for him at its end – Room 14's door stood open, waiting for him.

THE LOVERS

Epilogue

Brayden ran for the stairwell and hit the top landing with his heart pounding. Sweat prickled his scalp and made his shirt stick to the small of his back. His breath came in shallow, panting gasps before he even started to ascend.

The camera trembled in one hand as he gazed up at the landing of the next floor and shivered with a fear he couldn't quite name. "Fuck it," he said, shaking his head. "It's late. Let's get out while we can." His grin was forced as he moved a finger to shut off the recording.

With a final glance toward that unknown floor, he stowed his camera and started down. His planned speech from the top floor could be easily adjusted. He'd tell his followers something about the last floor. They'd believe him.

It probably *was* getting late, too. His watch had stopped working sometime before the third floor, and there weren't windows to see out – at least, not windows he trusted to look out on Chicago – but it had been hours, for sure.

In all his research, Brayden had never been able to learn exactly what time The Hyperion appeared every year, nor what time it disappeared. Just that it was gone in the morning. He didn't think it was close to morning yet, but still... time to go.

Stepping down onto the landing of the ninth floor, he heard the edge of the cackling that had left him screaming on the floor the last time he was there. He sped up, the cackles and screams in pursuit, gaining ground. Adrenaline spiked through his system.

Brayden descended through the building at a dead run, not sparing a single look at the corridors that had disgusted and terrified him. He jumped down the last several steps of every flight, often crashing into a balustrade or landing hard on a knee.

The cacophony filled Brayden's ears as he vaulted down the last flight and hit the ground running. He barged through the door into the lobby too fast for his momentum to keep him upright. Arms flailing, he lost his balance and skidded, spread-eagle, to the center of the lobby floor.

He bolted back up, running on pure adrenaline, crossed the lobby, and ran to the revolving door. One thought reverberated through his mind as he pushed the door.

"I survived the Hyperion! I survived the Hyperion! I survived the fucking Hyperion!"

Brayden Winchell pushed through the revolving door and entered the Hyperion.

Brayden Winchell went back through the revolving door and entered the Hyperion.

Brayden Winchell went through the revolving door and entered the Hyperion.

Brayden Winchell went back through the revolving door and entered the Hyperion.

He stood in the doorwell, staring at the lobby wide-eyed and open-mouthed in disbelief. He ran his fingers over the thirteen notches in his belt as he tried to make sense of it. He recited his unheard mantra as he did so.

He was done with this fucking place. It was time to go. What happened? His eyes fell on the desk. There was something there that hadn't been, before. Like a sleepwalker, he shuffled forward toward it.

The back of his head began to throb with every step. He could feel his pulse in his temples. His ears rang. He staggered as he neared the desk. Tears swam in his eyes, blurring his vision. He grabbed onto the desk to steady himself.

It was a manilla file folder. Written on its front in bold black marker were the words:

"The Sins of Brayden Winchell"

Brayden, hands trembling and eyes watering, began to page through the dossier.

The top of the first page read:

Victim one: Samantha Keats

Age: 22

And there she was, smiling for the camera in that sundress she wore, the day it all started. So young. So passionate about her singing. She'd make up a little song on the spot just because her milkshake was good. Fuck.

The next photo looked like a still from a security camera. There was Samantha in profile, perched on a bar stool, laughing and tipsy as she tried to eat a greasy pizza slice without staining her blousy white top. Brayden smiled in spite of himself, remembering.

The next one showed her hours later, mascara-smudged and exhausted, dozing in the passenger seat. Wind through the open windows had blown her hair around. One strand was stuck in her lipstick.

And then... after. Brayden swallowed, his breathing ragged. After the shouting. After the pleading. Long after he saw her laugh for the last time. He flipped through the rest of the photos, blinking rapidly. He hadn't meant... well, not really. Things... got out of hand.

One hand went to his belt, a fingernail flicking the edges of the first notch. Samantha. The first notch, though he didn't start that practice until after Morgan.

Brayden flipped a few pages.

Victim five: Diana Cain

Age: 24

Diana. Oh, Diana. Everything was a competition with her. If she couldn't make it a contest, she didn't want it. Brayden shook his head in fond exasperation. He flipped through the photos. In the last one, even in the state she was in, her eyes had that look. He half-expected the photo to speak, to say, "I win," one more time.

Brayden flipped a few more pages. His eye caught on the one he hated to remember. The one that almost brought his world crashing down. The scar she'd left on his neck stung, so much he had to check, to make sure it wasn't bleeding again.

Victim nine: Karen Talbot

Age: 29

There was a photo at the end that looked like it had been taken from across the street. It showed Brayden, exhausted and blood-covered, leaving the ER around dawn the next morning, a huge bandage on his neck. He had told them the wound was inflicted by a mugger. A few of them believed him. That one nurse wanted Brayden arrested. It was like she knew.

Trying to shake off the memory of the vengeful nurse, Brayden flipped through the rest of the dossier. They were all there. All of them. Their names, their ages, their pictures, their stories. All thirteen.

The folder fell from Brayden's numb hands, the pages scattering across the floor. His chest began to throb as his heart raced. He gripped the desk with both hands to stay up. He tasted blood at the back of his mouth.

He made his way around to the chair to sit down. A black suit was draped over it. On the lapel, a gold name tag read "Winchell." Brayden opened his mouth to protest, but a steady stream of blood turned the sound into a warbling cry. He fell to the floor and crawled on his hands and knees, moaning his drowned negation.

The blood began to run from his nose, from his eyes, his ears, streaming in ticklish rivulets down his neck. He reached up to touch an ache at the back of his head and found it wet, the surface pliant. He quickly pulled his hand away. It was drenched in blood.

Shit, that wasn't good. Brayden's mind was sluggish, searching for some way to make it out of this alive. Maybe one of the residents. Some of them were sort of nice. He pulled himself back to his feet with the aid of the desk and lurched to the wall.

From there, he started to inch toward the door into the stairwell. If he could make it somehow to the fifth floor, that guy was crazy, and he had those bugs, but he had the knowledge to patch Brayden up, and maybe tell him how to get out.

He rounded the corner already thinking about how he was going to cross the rubble in front of the elevators to get to the stairwell door. A backpack, just like his, lay among the rubble though it hadn't been there even a few minutes ago, when Brayden came bursting out of the stairwell.

A few feet away, a camera just like his lay shattered, a big chunk of ceiling debris at its center. Nearby, at the edge of the open elevator shaft, another big chunk was smeared with browning blood. Grateful for the momentary distraction, Brayden limped over to examine the broken camera.

The yawning danger of the shaft at his side whispered to him as he straightened painfully. He leaned over to have one more peek before starting his painful trek back up the stairs. There at the bottom, impaled neatly on the three wicked prongs he had noticed earlier, was the figure of a young man dressed just like himself.

With dawning horror, Brayden realized the figure was not just dressed like him. Somehow, it was his body down there. The back of his head oddly flat and matted with blood. He appeared to be dead.

Brayden's shrieks of denial echoed in the cavernous lobby. He covered his eyes, so he wouldn't have to see or accept the impossible evidence in front of them.

Whether he had screamed for a moment or an hour, when he opened his eyes again, he was behind the desk, in the suit, sitting in the chair.

He tried to scream again, but his lips were fused shut. All he could do was moan in the back of his throat. He found that his eyes were propped open, so he couldn't blink. As he watched, he could see at his cuffs that the suit was fusing to his skin. Twisting, he could see that the chair, in turn, was fused to the suit, making man, suit, and chair as one.

On the screens in front of him were the thirteen souls of The Hyperion – the ten whose stories he had heard and the three he had fled from in the halls. All of them were naked, in complete darkness. They writhed in anguish, tormented by unseen forces. Brayden couldn't look away.

A creeping fire like an army of fire ants began at his ankles and climbed steadily. Soon, every part of him covered by the horrible suit burned, and Brayden knew an agony he had never felt before. He would have writhed, had his attachment to the chair not rendered even that small freedom impossible.

From inside the manager's office came a low, booming laugh.

Brayden bowed his head to whimper in muffled agony until it was yanked upright by unseen hands. Where the revolving door had been was an open apartment door, angled so that it appeared he was on the inside. The gold numbers read, "14."

The door began to creak closed. Brayden thrashed, trying desperately to force out muffled screams as it slammed shut, enclosing The Hyperion's newest resident.

Kickstarter Wall of Impish Appreciation

A.L. Garcia	Alex J. Holmes
Alexis Hilgert	Amanda Laughton
Andrew Morgan	Anne C.
Anonymous C	Anthony LaFauci
Aristophanes Cedeño	Ashleigh Floyd
Bre Crosby	Bryan C. Miles
Caroline Coriell	Colin Dagnall
Dewi Hargreaves	Doc Bradshaw
Douglas Noreen	E.M. Wallace
Elle McIntosh	Erin Fagan
Heidi Halstead	Jae Margal
James Morgan	Jess Leigh
Joseph George	Kat and Eric
Lane Foster	Mary Vásquez
Matthew Siadak	Mia Vásquez
Nikki Crump-Hanstead	PD Austin
RT Slaywood	Ryan Christy
S.C. Morgan	Tad K
Tea With Coffee Media	The Oracular Beard
William Lahaie	

Acknowledgements

With all our whimsically dark hearts, we want to thank the Twitter Writing Community, where this idea was first conceived, where the editors met, and where we met most of our collaborators, as well as many of our supporters, both financial and moral. Every comment, every retweet, every tagging of someone you thought would be interested – it all helped build the book you hold in your hands. Anyone who says internet communities aren't real is woefully misinformed, to begin with, but also, has never seen the magic of *our* community. May we never lose sight of that magic.

Whatever the future holds for our community, on whatever platform(s), we love and appreciate you, and hope we have many more years watching and supporting each other as we weave stories and chase dreams.

Thanks also to all of the talented storytellers and poets who submitted to the project and entrusted us with work to be considered for inclusion. We read every submission together, in time though not geography, and were keenly aware of the privilege we were being offered as we considered each piece. This volume is made of that work entrusted to us and could not exist without it.

Thank you so much to the friends, family, and strangers who offered the financial support we needed to pay our contributors, which was an important goal for the project, commission the gorgeous floorplan we have included at the front of the book, and deliver a beautiful, professional book to serve as a suitable presentation of every piece inside.

Special thanks to Jessica Laymon and @KTinDC, hosts of the #fastprompt challenge where The Hyperion's origin story dawned; to F.K. Marlowe, for her unstinting enthusiasm throughout and her invaluable eleventh-hour feedback in the creation of the cover; to Bryan C. Miles and Laura Cooney, for their infectious enthusiasm from the very first day we announced the project; to Juliet Wilde, for her valuable, clear-eyed feedback; and to Jared Conti, The Oracular Beard, for his support and feedback, his keen eye, and his uncanny knack for knowing when someone needs to hear, "Hey, you're doing great. You've got this."

A profound thank you to the loved ones – found family as much as blood, real as much as imagined – who have shaped us and supported us, who have listened to our stories, who have helped us stand when we've faltered, who have endured late-night tip-tapping on keys, and who have smiled with pride to see us fly. You are, each of you, imbued with your own special magic.

To the toddler banging away on a Fisher-Price typewriter on the living room floor who informed an inquiring mother that the document being typed was an essay on Esther Tusquets, and the kindergartner stretched out on the floor creating Sherlock Holmes picture books (featuring Victorian helicopters, of course) as soon as eyeglasses made it possible to see the page – we're so glad you kept writing.

And to you, our "constant reader," as Mr. King would have it, ***thank you***.